ELECTION:

DEZINFORMATSIYA

AND THE GREAT

GAME

Chris Graham

ISBN: 0692252282
ISBN 13: 9780692252284
Library of Congress Control Number: 2014912504
Sapphire Group, Destin FL

DEDICATION

For The Monkey, The Tomato, The Banana, Po
and all true friends.

This book was inspired by the strategies revealed in: *We Will Bury You* by Major General Jan Sejna, *Disinformation* by Lieutenant General Ion Pacepa, *Comrade J* by Pete Earley, *Unrestricted Warfare* by Colonel Qiao Liang and Colonel Wang Xiangsui and *An Explanatory Memorandum* by Mohamed Akram. This book is a work of fiction.

"It must be said, that like the breaking of a great dam, the American descent into Marxism is happening with breath taking speed…" – Stanislav Mishin, *Pravda*, 27 April 2009

1.

U.S. EMBASSY ANNEX

BENGHAZI, LIBYA

9:40 P.M.

11 SEPTEMBER 2012

Ambassador Chris Stevens was closing the door to his bedroom and trying to remember the pronunciation of a Turkish phrase he had attempted to use an hour or so earlier. As he pressed the door closed an earth shattering boom sent an instantaneous wave of icy dread through his body. As the items in the room rattled momentarily he recovered from stumbling and clumsily fingered the door lock.

A rocket propelled grenade (RPG) hit the front gate of the small compound. The Libyan Supreme Security Council (SSC) guard stationed at the main gate had already dropped his baseball bat and fled. SSC was a name given to local militia members that the State Department was paying for unarmed security.

Chris Stevens was in the Ambassador's Villa, Sean Smith, another State employee, was playing a video game in another room. Four Diplomatic Security Service (DSS) agents were in their villa and a fifth was on duty in the small Tactical Operations Center (TOC). Four more security guards hired from the February 17 Martyrs Brigade dropped their bats and ran into the villas fleeing the gate.

For a moment Steven's fear flashed to indignant anger. The "Annex" complex they were in had appalling security. He had requested appropriate security time after time; even once in person when briefing the Secretary of State. He knew Benghazi's SETL (Security Environment Threat List) score. He knew funds had been appropriated to cover this.

He desperately wished that he had a WPS (Worldwide Protective Service) team like the one he had in Jerusalem, but instead of contracted Marine and Ranger combat veterans he was being protected by Diplomatic Security Service employees. He was proud that they resembled a 'diversity' poster, but he had to admit that he now found himself wondering what combat experience they had. They were good people though, and he *hoped* they had a plan to evacuate successfully.

The DSS agent on duty in the TOC could see dozens of men with AK-47s and RPGs entering the compound through the main gate. He noticed one had a PKM belt fed machinegun. Most of the shooting in the compound was in the air; there just wasn't anyone to shoot. The TOC agent sounded the alarm over the radio and called the Embassy in Tripoli for help. Then he called the nearby Benghazi CIA annex. In a panicked voice, he said, "We're under attack, we need help, please send help now..." The line went dead. They were outnumbered and outgunned.

One of the other DSS agents went to the ambassador's villa and told Stevens and Smith to put on their body armor. She then led them to a room she hoped would be more secure in the back of the building. She locked the door and radioed the TOC. The agent was armed with an M4, Sig and a Remington 870, but she hoped against hope that the attacking militia might back off. She had never been in combat before and was afraid she might provoke them if she fired.

Stevens demanded the agents' cell phone and since she didn't have a better idea she gave it to him. The ambassador began making calls to Tripoli for help. They both listened to the attackers firing and destroying everything in their path room by room.

One of the remaining DSS agents ran to the TOC. The other two, withdrew in the face of the onslaught and barricaded themselves in a separate villa with one of the February 17 guards.

The attacking militia found fuel containers and torched several vehicles in the compound. They entered the ambassador's villa, destroying and looting its contents. Then they found the locked door the Americans were hidden behind. After unsuccessful attempts to batter the door down they poured diesel fuel into the room. Soon a raging, toxic fire was underway.

Steven's villa was immersed in a thick cloud from burning fuel and tires and the Americans crawled into one of the bathrooms. The gasping agent opened the window, but it sucked smoke in at an alarming rate. Visibility in the room was zero. The agent yelled to Stevens, but they had become separated in the chaos. Staying inside would be death.

The agent made it out of the building and ducked away from a flurry of machinegun fire. She went back into the building, but found only militants. She broke several windows trying to get air for Stevens and Smith and then called for help. The looting then overtook the compound, but the TOC and the villa safe room were secure.

Outside the State Department compound, two Toyota Land Cruisers slowed to a more subtle pace, closed the last couple of blocks and quietly parked against the back wall. Six fit, but scruffy Westerners got out. Their nostrils were assaulted with the acrid smell of burning rubber and pollution. They were armed with short barrel HK 416s, and Glocks. Two had Para-SAW machineguns and one had an HK69 grenade launcher. They parked close to the compound wall, locked the vehicles and climbed on them to climb over. Nobody fired a shot until the small team was set in an L-shaped ambush formation.

Ty, a former SEAL, called the DSS TOC on a local cellphone and told them not to fire on his guys. Then all hell broke loose. Ty's team of former SEAL and Force Recon CIA contractors unleashed everything they had on the marauders. The team soon had the attackers on the run. One of the former Marines lobbed 40 millimeter grenades into clusters of fleeing militia. Each pocket blown up increased the amount of time the militants would need to reset to resume their attack. One of the SEALs picked up a bloody PKM from beneath a throng of bodies and sent hundreds of enemy rounds into the temporarily routed militia. Within minutes, the small team had turned the tide: dead enemy littered the compound, and the rest were running for cover.

The team maneuvered their way to some of the DSS agents. During a lull in fire, the remaining agents in the outlying villa joined up with the main element. The State agents were ill-prepared to be of much help, so instead of recapturing and holding the compound the CIA crew sent the DSS team back to the CIA compound while they stayed to look for the ambassador. Ty signaled for the team to move to the main TOC building while the State Department employees hurriedly left in their armored vehicles.

Small arms fire was picking up again, and the team shot their way to the ambassador's burning building as several RPGs exploded nearby. They located Smith. He was on the ground, unconscious and had no pulse. They continued searching for the ambassador but eventually had to break off their efforts. The compound would be completely overrun by enemy forces eventually and they needed to break out before that happened. They no longer had the element of surprise working for them and their ammo was running low. They radioed that there was no sign of the ambassador and they were on their way back.

They shot their way back to the armored Land Cruisers with two captured enemy machineguns. The team braved heavy rocket fire and AK–47s the entire way. The rest of the guys returned fire with well-aimed 5.56 shots—making each remaining round count. Once inside the vehicle they called back to base, "Five minutes out." Their cars were rattled by small arms fire, their tires flattened and their bullet resistant windows were filled with the spider web cracks that come from led projectiles being embedded at high velocity. "One minute out," they called.

The gate closed behind them just before midnight. Ty was relieved to see the Chief of Station (COS) welcome them back. Despite not having military combat experience he had argued the smart commander's perspective: "leave the annex to those State morons!" He did not want to see his six boys leaping into oblivion in a doomed attempt to save others from their own incompetent bosses. Ironically, Ty had made the emotional argument that they too were Americans. Ty also happened to have the Land Cruiser keys in his pocket.

Meanwhile, the militia leaders repositioned their forces for an attack on the CIA base. Here, however, the militants ran into machinegun positions manned by well screened, well paid and well trained Libyans. Waves of enemy were KIA.

Before sunup a private jet carrying a sister team from Tripoli landed in Benghazi. This second U.S. team had had to bluster their way onboard the aircraft and deliver a bag of cash to finally inspire cooperation, but they made it. They eventually harassed their way through the Benghazi airport and joined the fight just after 5:00 a.m. Minutes after their vehicle drove through the gate the base came under heavy fire again. The seven new guys were quick to take up defensive positions. Several of the enemy tried coming over the wall, but were shot.

Ty was on the rooftop manning a Para-SAW with two others when Glen, a SEAL from the Tripoli team climbed onto the roof. The two friends embraced as brothers quickly filling each other in.

The attackers had been firing mortars off and on. Now at least one of their mortar teams was employing a technique common to experienced and well trained crews. They were bracketing; firing one round long, another short, then halving the elevation adjustments. The rounds were getting closer with each shot.

BOOM! Ty's position was hit with a French 81mm mortar round, fatally wounding the man. Ty's body shielded another—saving the man's life, though still leaving him seriously wounded. As Glen attempted to reposition and take cover, a second round impacted, killing him instantly.

Putting themselves at risk, several more operators ran up to the roof to assist. Their quick action saved two men's lives. They lowered the bodies down with a fast-rope they had pulled out of the Cross Fit gym. One wounded man made it down the ladder with a wounded agent on his back under a hail of incoming fire.

A JSOC (Joint Special Operations Command) operator was monitoring the situation on his handheld ROVER, a device used to display pod data from aircraft. He was watching a Predator feed from overhead. It was an unarmed UAV (unmanned aerial vehicle) equipped with multiple sensors that could detect infrared (IR) and thermal signatures. The drone had been redirected to the scene by the DOD's AFRICOM (Africa Command) at the request of the JSOC operator. Few elements could have physically made it to the Americans in time to help, and those that could have unsurprisingly were not dispatched as stove-piped bureaucracies struggled to figure out how to quickly authorize sensitive assets from one agency to assist another agency's shadowy project in a different country and different theater of operations. Nothing less than a direct order from the President could have had a chance of getting the ball rolling in time.

"There's a large element assembling, and we need to get everyone out of here now!" the JSOC man relayed to the COS. The images on the ROVER's screen was enough to convince the CIA Chief. They immediately notified everyone to gather their security items and evacuate.

Within minutes of the decision, the vehicles were loaded and the Americans were on their way to the airport. They encountered small arms fire on the way but arrived unscathed in time to meet the first of two aircraft that would fly them back to Tripoli. The handful of Americans had rescued State Department employees, killed nearly 100 attackers out of a company sized paramilitary force armed with AK-47s and supported by belt fed machine guns, RPGs and mortars and scrupulously sterilized their sensitive items before withdrawing.

After touching down in Tripoli, the Benghazi station chief walked into a conference room with cable news playing on a television at the head of the table. Still prints of the action taken from Benghazi security camera feeds were being passed around. Two faces had been positively identified so far- one from al Qaeda in the Islamic Maghreb (AQIM), one from al Qaeda in the Arabian Peninsula (AQAP).

On the television the US Ambassador to the United Nations was speaking with an interviewer. She confirmed Ambassador Stevens had been killed and continued, "…our current best assessment, based on the information that we have at present, is that, in fact, what this began as, it was a spontaneous — not a premeditated — response to this very offensive video, as you know, a few hours earlier, there was a violent protest that was undertaken in reaction to an offensive video that was disseminated."

"What the hell is she smoking?!" the chief bellowed at the screen. Why didn't the President launch the Marine team in Italy? What video was she talking about? Why was the ambassador to the U.N. speaking instead of the President or Secretary of State? There was no protest.

1.01

WALL STREET

NEW YORK, NEW YORK

6:40 P.M.

16 DECEMBER 1974

Nick Sludtsev sat behind his desk contorted to look through the window as far as he could see. He was far from the top floors, but he could see the wisps of smoke and steam outside confirming it was still just as frigid as it was when he came in. He was feeling particularly uninspired. He fidgeted and rummaged through the sloppily folded New York Times on his desk. Life was out of balance. He knew he was a winner, but he didn't feel like he had evidence to prove it at the moment.

Nick had been scraping, struggling, and clawing his way forward his whole life. He had been born outside Moscow in a different time. A tougher time. Stalin's people considered his lineage to be Jewish and his father was a businessman and a property owner. He wasn't wealthy, but any of those facts could have gotten him killed. Nick learned how to keep his head down and survive.

When the peasants were able to label someone a *kulak,* or property owner, and have their possessions taken from them, Mr. Sludtsev began planning. By the time Stalin's Jewish pogroms were up and running the father had seen the writing on the wall. Generations of Russian rulers had targeted Jews when they needed an enemy to unify the remainder of the population, when they needed someone to steal from or when they just had a sadistic urge to kick someone around.

Mr. Sludtsev bribed a nearby apparatchik to take his boy in. Young Nick became the "visiting nephew" and Mr. Sludtsev lowered his profile, took a government job and became an outspoken proponent of Joseph Stalin. Nick's new 'father' figure enjoyed a double win. He gained a supplementary off-the-books paycheck and he gained a young assistant to groom and help in his duties. The boy carried out the tasks he was assigned without complaining regardless of how cold it was outside. Nick was a survivor.

By the end of The War, Mr. Sludtsev had just a little 'pull' in his local piece of Stalin's government and he had saved enough rubles to give his boy one last gift. Nick's father understood that any bureaucracy is a collection of people with their hands out, and he knew from the experience of the previous years that the bigger that bureaucracy was, the more hands would be out.

All he had to do was find the right hand. The right hand would provide the paperwork necessary to spirit his boy out of Russia and the wrong hand would put them both and Nick's mother in a Siberian Gulag for 'counter-revolutionary activities'. Father had to pick the hand that valued an honest bribe and possibly the thrill of defying the all-powerful State over the hand that preferred to receive crumbs for informing on his neighbors. Father knew the latter well. The former might only have been a fantasy if not for his perceptive eye and patient manner.

In 1949 Mr. Sludtsev succeeded in shipping his boy off for a better life. Young Nick was received in New York by his uncle. At first, America was both a terror and a wonder. The young man was flexible though and adapted without any lasting troubles. His life, like everyone else's at the mercy of Stalin's whims, created internal questions. Nick was intrigued by power. Who got to make the rules? Why them? Economics seemed to be a good fit and it permitted him to pursue answers to those two questions. In 1954 he successfully earned a degree from New York University's School of Economics.

The young man gratefully accepted an entry level position at a trading house and before long he deftly made a lateral move into arbitrage. He found elements of the work to be fascinating. The numbers were his tools and with them he could build a new universe. Before the end of the decade he was a portfolio manager. He spent a couple of years gaining additional insight as an analyst. But it had become clear early on where he had to go.

In 1974 Nick was working on Wall Street and living in Greenwich Village. Something in the Americans' manner was off-putting to him. Americans were brash and freely shared convictions based on near-total historical ignorance of the world. And yet there was something magical about the time and place too. Nick knew that this was where he would begin his journey to change the world. Hell, the United Nations, possibly the world's best, maybe only, hope to elevate the... condition of mankind... had offices here.

He had managed a hedge fund and like everybody on Wall Street, part of him wanted to man the helm of his own ship. He knew he could do it. He knew he was smarter than the others. The question was how? He didn't pick winners any better than anybody else did and he consistently made enemies at a one-for-one pace with the number of allies he made.

It was enough to give a man a migraine, but here he sat waiting for a call back from a man that seemed to be a candidate for becoming a useful ally. He had met Philip Montaigne nearly a year ago. As precise as he was, he couldn't remember exactly how they had met, but he seemed rather bland until not too long ago when he was able to be of assistance. Philip was able to share some useful information with him. He let him know how much wheat was going to be ordered by a contact in Germany, and on what schedule, days before anyone else could read the signs and figure it out.

While this information was a little afield his primary concerns, he was able to capitalize on it. In fact if he were honest with himself he had to admit that a little piece of his genius was Philip's cleverness or at least the collective value of all of his contacts including Philip.

Best of all, Philip had intrigued him with the possibility of a joint venture that sounded exciting.

When the phone finally rang, he scooped the receiver up and put it to the side of his head. Playing with the green curly phone cord he opened his end of the conversation with "Philip, how are you?" when he heard his friend's greeting.

They bantered briefly, but something was wrong. He was bending a kink in the cord around the cradle when Philip gave him the news. "I discussed the venture we talked about with my partners, but they are not interested in moving forward…Nick, I'm sorry." He sounded like he was genuinely surprised by the bad news.

1.02

THE CENTER

YASENEVO, MOSCOW

4:46 P.M.

4 JANUARY 1975

KGB Chairman Yuri Andropov was a man many found intimidating. He could be fiery and unexpected, if only to keep others off guard. He was also a shrewd and calculating man. Not only had he survived The War years and the various purges, but he managed to rise to the top. Those closest to him were convinced his star was still on the rise. One did not achieve these things without having a highly honed ability to anticipate, mold and create unending layers of ancillary causes and effects. Chairman Andropov's mind was a chessboard with an infinite number of pieces to orchestrate.

Andropov was on that chessboard. He sat at the head of a carved table with a couple of directorate chiefs, a few deputies and two more logistics officers. Part of The Chairman's mind registered Igor's words.

Igor, a man known in the cables as *Comrade Kray,* was discussing some of the outgrowths of OPERATION SIG. All members of the Warsaw Pact recognized the United States as 'The Main Enemy'. America was the primary, maybe only, significant obstacle to stand in the way of the dawn of global socialism. A universal dictatorship of the proletariat may or may not materialize, but someone would be the dominant power and the people of Russia rewarded Chairman Andropov very well to make sure it would be the Communist Party of the Soviet Union.

America's center-of-gravity, as the army called it, was her productivity. The country had abundant natural resources, a skilled workforce, the premier, though greying, industrial infrastructure in the world and an inspiring ideology. Refugees came from around the world for a chance to make a better life. In exchange for admission they were expected to learn English, assimilate and be productive. The Chairman understood Americans called this concept the 'Melting Pot'.

The great challenge in this competition was the way decisions were made. For the Soviets to wield power, there had to be a strong central decision making body or decision maker. If not, regardless of the principles of Democratic Socialism, they could never be more than a rabble without direction. Americans on the other hand believed in the 'Invisible Hand'. The Chairman knew that most Americans had never heard of the invisible hand, but they certainly understood how it worked.

Each American was free to create and produce according to his own initiative. Decisions of production were in private hands. Whoever produced and delivered the best for the least would be rewarded by an army of individual consumers.

Of course, that system was entirely unfair. It was chaotic and barbaric and the First Secretary had ordered him to find its' vulnerabilities and exploit them. The current First Secretary of the Central Committee was not the first to give that order, and this Chairman was not the first chairman to receive it.

The KGB did what all intelligence services did. One of those tasks was collecting information. All information was not equal of course, so The Center prioritized. The more needed the information was, and the more difficult to obtain, the more it was prized. The Chairman knew the KGB had an edge. The entire Party knew the value of this information and budgeted accordingly. The KGBs network was the largest intelligence network in the world. From full-fledged collection officers from each Warsaw Pact country down to an army of 'fellow travelers' helping the cause and people in useful positions around the world that could be motivated to help, there were very few places The Chairman could not place a set of friendly ears.

The KGB also provided security at home, and that took diligence to oversee, but that wasn't the 'Great Game'. Layer one that every man in this room knew about was that The Chairman had officers in all the embassies of Warsaw Pact countries. Not too long ago it occurred to The Chairman that if this war heated up, he might be in jeopardy of having his most productive collectors rolled up simultaneously. Blindness was not acceptable, so he created a second layer.

The second layer had no signature to catch. The KGB had a network of men who had been trained as collectors, then trained as diplomats. They were placed at embassies and other non-state offices throughout the world. They were entirely dormant, standing ready to be activated on command. That prevented the possibility of catastrophic blindness, but The Chairman didn't play chess not to lose. He played to win.

Comrade Kray boomed, momentarily capturing The Chairman's attention again. "SIG [Sionistskiye Gosudarstra, or Operation Zionist Governments] has met two-thirds of the bench marks set". OPERATION ARES had been quite successful in bleeding the American's zeal in Vietnam with some well-placed *dezinformatsiya* (disinformation) credibly circulated through world news services, and a relatively small financial investment washed through various front groups and into the pockets of the most virulent anti-war activists. SIG was The Chairman's multi-year initiative to create friction for NATO in general and the United States in particular in the Arab world. Of course, it had to be bigger and better than ARES. *The Protocols of the Elders of Zion* was translated and had new life breathed into it. The fabricated document explaining the Jewish/ American conspiracy to take over the world was given new legs in the Mideast and central to the remaining one-third of SIG's objectives, a charismatic Egyptian revolutionary and 'fellow traveler' named: Mohammed

Yasser Abdel Rahman Abdel Raouf Arafat al-Qudwa al-Husseini, had been put through one of the KGBs special operations schools and was built into Palestinian Abu Ammar. The world press was calling him Yasser Arafat.

The Chairman placed his water glass back on the table and gave his consent to supplement the portfolio of ongoing activities with OPERATION TAYFUN [Typhoon]. Now, instead of just insinuating disinformation into influential Western sources, and stoking the ambitions of collegiate Che Guevaras, funds had been dedicated to support a revolutionary war. The KGB had seen to it that the Red Brigades, the Baader-Meinhoff Gang, the Popular Front for the Liberation of Palestine, the Palestinian Liberation Organization, revolutionaries in Iran and a host of others received indoctrination, and training in East Germany, Yemen and a couple of other carefully guarded destinations.

Now The Chairman wanted to see a return on his investment. Pin pricks around the world were unimpressive. He wanted surveillance ramped up. He wanted these groups' target lists approved. He wanted to see a typhoon across Europe and the Mideast that would sap economies and test NATO alliances.

What nobody in this room knew, however, was that The Chairman was prepared to open a third layer of KGB initiatives. Today he would tell *Comrade Cardinal* to proceed.

1.03

GREENWICH VILLAGE
NEW YORK, NEW YORK
9:50 P.M.
12 JANUARY 1975

John Gardner glanced left and right to make sure the street was clear and stepped off the curb. A gust ruffled his blond hair and in moments he was indistinguishable in the evening foot traffic. At 5'7" he was identical to the crowd's median height. His grey-blue eyes moved actively but subtly, scanning details. He was in the moment, and every cell of his being was alive.

John had spent exactly nine minutes at the coffee shop he just left. That had been necessary to get his timing back on schedule. His journey may have been nearly six hours long, but his arrival had to be precise. Now that he was *on*, he was free to make his next stop. He walked into the narrow drugstore at the corner and purchased a 'Times'. Getting a good view through the front window he was able to see the crowd that had been behind him without turning his head. Dropping his change on the counter he was back on the street, took a corner and walked into the cinema with a ticket he already had.

Mr. Gardner flowed with the crowd to the right. Despite the throng, his auditorium had no line. He was just a minute earlier than people arrived for his show and he walked straight in. As he moved to the fire exit he placed his hat in a pocket, and removed his rain coat. Nobody followed him in and each of the three people inside; a couple on the far side, and a lone man at the top were there before he came in.

He knew the door would not alarm from the report he had read. When he was out the other side of the building he paused momentarily putting the raincoat back on- reversed to a different pattern. He re-wrapped his scarf with a different colored side now showing, pulled on a knit cap from a different pocket and slid on a set of non-magnified wire rim eyeglasses as he stepped out of the alcove. He believed he was 'clean' and he walked deliberately and directly to the poetry reading at the coffeehouse to his front.

When Nick Sludtsev walked in after mere minutes elapsed, he headed back to the private booth that Philip Montaigne told him to go to weeks previously. Nick looked at John for the first time, but sat as though he knew him just as he had been instructed. John smiled and greeted him familiarly, all the while assessing him through eyes that could warm up only to impassionate. God only knew how cold they could get.

Nick was confident. He had knowingly made illegal transactions based on information that Philip had given him to the benefit of several hundred percent. He knew he had crossed a line. It was not by accident. George was willing to do what others would not do so that he could live as others could not live. He was not going to try to outguess every competitor, every transaction every day, for the rest of his life. He wanted inside information and he had consciously made the decision to do what was required to obtain a steady stream of it.

"Nikolay" John said using Nick's given name, "I am prepared to provide everything Philip offered you." He let that sink in while studying the man. After a pause he added slowly…"All you have to do is assist Mother Russia"… John stared intently at the man, convinced his skills were so highly developed that he could take the measure of a source from a single conversation.

Nick's blood ran cold, but the KGB had not failed to do its' homework. The Center's psychologists had studied all of the open source data on Sludtsev. They read every report "Philip" had filed from the Form 21A from when they first "happened" to meet, to the transcripts of every word the target had uttered to his "friend". They dissected Sludtsev's book on economics and found it interesting that he referenced a need to "manage" the economy.

They went through the archives and studied Nick's father's NKVD source reports. They considered the young man's experience assisting the State in property seizure and distributing leaflets that told property owners and Jews where to report for 'relocation'. They liked what they saw. The psychological report asserted that Sludtsev could be convinced that he was being given the opportunity to redeem his family's name performing a critically important service that only he could provide to Mother Russia.

He was assessed to need wealth, but his single dominant motivating force was the quest for power. They believed this would continue to grow over time. The report also described Sludtsev's belief in right and wrong to be an assessment of what helped him get what he wanted. That which was immoral was that which did not serve his purpose. The man was assessed at the highest level of potential for recruitment as a source.

Over the course of their conversation the men agreed that the Soviet Union would provide Sludtsev with seed money to launch his own fund and the KGB would provide him information that would give him an edge. In return all Nikolay had to do was set up a philanthropic foundation with a percentage of his proceeds and use it as John directed.

Sludtsev departed first. A few minutes later John walked out. John returned to the movie theater alcove, returned his clothing to its' original appearance and joined the crowd filtering out the exit of his movie. He made his way to the Canadian border and at the height of morning traffic made his way to Ottawa International Airport.

John was freshly graduated from The Institute. His father had smoothed the way for his acceptance. His athletic performance, ratings on tactical drills and tradecraft was superior. However, his academic performance was dead-average, his intellect was scored above the population average, but at the median for his class. His classmates thought of him as something of a thug. *Comrade Cardinal* was elated to have been requested by The Chairman for a special assignment.

Halfway through training at The Institute, he had witnessed his senior instructor rundown a woman while in a vodka induced fog. When uniformed security services personnel interviewed him he said he did not see the hit and run driver or his plates. He never spoke of it to his fellow students or institute staff. "John" was never informed that the incident was a hoax. His mediocrity would mean that his classmates weren't watching him in the competition for glory. His ability to perform and keep his mouth shut marked him as one of the men The Chairman wanted for his new initiative.

Comrade Cardinal had gone on from the Institute to an unglamorous posting in the Second Chief Directorate (Counter Intelligence) in Dresden, East Germany and none of his classmates gave him a second thought. While tacitly holding this billet, he spent weeks and months isolated being trained in perfect American English, history, mannerisms and customs. He spent hours on end with people who had lived in the USA and watched American movies and television every day. Every few weeks he was assessed by psychologists from The Center. The Chairman was afraid so much American entertainment would sap the man's intellect.

Nikolay had the highest level of anonymity. There was no Dossier of Recruitment. 'Philip Montaigne', his recruiting officer from the New York *rezidentura*, believed that The Center assessed him to be a CIA dangle and ordered that recruitment efforts be broken off. There would be no cables for prying eyes to read detailing Nikolay's work. From here on out Nikolay would be known as *Comrade Pike*. The Chairman ran *Comrade Cardinal, Comrade Cardinal* ran *Comrade Pike* and no others were in the loop.

In days, *Comrade Cardinal* would have changed from John Gardner into Dieter Munzinger and flown from Ottawa to London, London to Berlin and made his way to stand before The Chairman. He looked forward to proudly reporting that *Comrade Pike* would already be underway submitting filings to launch the Magna-Stellar Fund under Sludtsev Enterprises, LLC on Madison Avenue in Manhattan.

1.04

"**...A**nd when we return…Dr. Carl Sagan… with a warning that will knock your socks off!" A man with thick grey hair, and wire glasses bantered with his studio audience. He guided them skillfully and they responded to his every gesture. He had the ability to flare his eyes into what an ex-girlfriend once called his "indignant bug eyes" while simultaneously condescending, discussing an idea he expected his audience to find ridiculous, then he would back off and the conversational tension would be relieved. It was a recipe that had seen his television career ascend from a local Ohio market to national syndication.

Dr. Sagan walked through a faux-wood door placarded "Donahue" and stepped on stage to applause. Both men sat. Greetings were exchanged and the interviewer demanded, "Tell me about... Nuclear... Winter" speaking haltingly for dramatic effect.

Over the next 10 minutes, Dr. Sagan spoke with just a few interruptions to elicit more details. A horrified audience listened to a modern Armageddon story. If there were a nuclear exchange in Europe even if limited in scope to the minimum necessary to repel a Soviet land forces invasion of Germany, so much earth and debris would be blown into the atmosphere that the particles would block out the sun providing continuous darkness. This darkness would cause global temperatures to plummet. An ice age might ensue. At a minimum, food crops would be destroyed and millions would die slowly and unpleasantly. Sagan repeated this warning on TV shows, radio shows and in lectures across the country. Unknown scientists and academics around the world endeavored to follow in his footsteps. But the story did not begin there.

Chairman Andropov had savored the reports of OPERATION TAYFUN's successes over the past years. Revolutionary groups across Europe, the Mideast and much of the rest of the world were striking the imperialist capitalists. Tel Aviv and Jerusalem were echoing from Palestinian bombs and Europeans were once again forced to hold their breath after a number of attacks. NATO facilities were bombed across Europe and NATO officers were targeted for assassination or kidnapping.

Pleased with the discord he was sowing among those who had been tempted to experiment with 'The American Model' or get cozy with the United States, he set his sights higher still. At the same time The Chairman's typhoon was blowing around the world, Directorate "A" disinformation operations continued as usual. KGB forgers created "incriminating" documents to disseminate through unwitting, but receptive reporters as well as paid assets. Activist groups that advanced socialism or agitated for policies that would cause political and financial strife in capitalist countries were surreptitiously shown favor. Whether advocating for disarmament, environmental regulation that would inhibit Western productivity or any other radical cause that could be boosted, the most productive groups could count on well-laundered clandestine stipends.

The Chairman also saw the opportunity for a more cogent effort. By 1979 *Comrade Pike's* Magna-Stellar Fund was a 100 million dollar enterprise and he had successfully launched the Free Community Partnership (FCP) and by 1983 Magna-Stellar was up to 500 million. FCP had created several pass-through entities to disburse funds to allies that were able to advance the revolution. Not with guns and bombs, at least not here, not now, but through ideology and through agitation for policy. He even had channels opened to both American political parties and minor streams of assistance to key progressive figures in each. The best part was it cost nothing. With nothing more than inside information provided by the world's largest intelligence organization, Magna-Stellar was outperforming all other funds. Of course to stay below the peak and out of the spotlight a large volume of funds was diverted through networks parallel to FCP. Anything that advanced an agenda that could discredit the free-market concept or the value of the individual received assistance. These were just drops in the bucket and none were expected to change the world over night, but they did add up.

The Warsaw Pact also faced challenges. The United States and NATO had decided to deploy Pershing II nuclear missiles throughout Europe. This would blunt the tremendous numerical advantage of the Warsaw Pact's ground forces. The Chairman was not a man who would sit idle while advantages were squandered.

At his direction, the Institute of Terrestrial Physics of the Soviet Academy of Sciences made the Kondrayev Discovery. Geophysicist Gersi Golitsyn, mathematician N.N. Moiseyev, and computer scientist V.V. Aleksandrov refined a theoretical model that allowed them to calculate the amount of debris that would be blown into the atmosphere under a range of potential nuclear exchanges in Europe. Under the watchful eye of Yuri Israel, Chairman of the USSR State Committee for Hydro-Meteorology and Environmental Control they input Kondrayev's "anti-hothouse effect" and they came to a staggering conclusion.

Only there was no experimentation. There was no application of the scientific method. The Chairman simply told his 'scientists' what he wanted, and they published their findings.

The "scientific foundations" sponsored by *Comrade Pike's* Free Community Partnership were among the first to receive the Academy of Sciences paper. Each did their job and passed it on to their press contacts and scientists around the world began hypothesizing based on the foundation of these findings. Skeptical scientists had to contemplate whether it was worth being seen as endorsing nuclear war to question the scientific validity of these doomsday claims.

Meanwhile, on an overcast Chicago day, a television studio audience and the army of voting spectators watching from home were educated on the threat of 'Nuclear Winter'. Dr. Carl Sagan, America's best known astronomer, opened the eyes of many thousands of viewers. Other writers, speakers and entertainers combined to open the eyes of millions. The fact that the scientific method was not employed to prove the cataclysmic Nuclear Winter predictions did not make it any less "scientific" in the minds of those informed. The Pershing II missile would never be deployed as widely as the Americans had intended.

1.05

STATE DACHA

OUTSIDE MOSCOW

10:10 P.M.

7 JANUARY 1983

General Secretary Yuri Andropov poured another few fingers of his personal vodka into a clear glass and handed it to the man in front of him. Now that all three men were topped off they could resume their toasts. Ironically, the only man of the three wearing a formal Soviet military officer's uniform was an American citizen.

KGB Chairman Andropov had been extremely pleased with Nikolay Sludtsev's efforts. His enterprise was highly influential; it was a significant part of the reason he had risen to General Secretary and best of all, this enterprise paid for itself. *Comrade Cardinal* reported that *Comrade Pike* had taken pride in the very important role he was playing in service of the Union of Soviet Socialist Republics and made a very unusual suggestion.

As a result of that suggestion, the General Secretary of the Communist Party of the Soviet Union, and a KGB case officer- both in suits that had long since been relaxed- sat before a flickering fireplace with an American citizen wearing the uniform of a Russian lieutenant colonel.

"You have done very well" the General Secretary complimented. Lieutenant Colonel Sludtsev's uniform was adorned with each medal that he was- just this evening- told that he had earned over the years. *Comrade Cardinal* felt confident that this gesture and private ceremony would strengthen Sludtsev's commitment and resolve. He was confident they could demand even more of him now.

It was clear that Sludtsev understood that men needed to be led. The idea of each man personally making the choices that determined his own destiny was naïve and foolish if one intended for mankind to progress. Sludtsev could also be counted on to follow power. As the enterprise grew, there had been no opportunity to micromanage what he was doing *and* keep their relationship secret. His instincts had proven excellent and he had grown his own networks of 'fellow travelers' capable of wielding influence and making wise use of the funds the Free Community Partnership received from the Magna-Stellar Fund. Sludtsev was amassing Wall Street wealth and power all the while advancing the agenda of his Soviet partners. International travel was of course standard and he was even able to use his contacts for commercial access behind the Iron Curtain that few others could pull off. This was in fact his third visit to Moscow in as many years. This was his first meeting with The General Secretary. This was his first meeting with *Comrade Cardinal* here.

The General Secretary went on to inflate *Comrade Pike's* ego, "Nikolay I must tell you the purpose...the point of it all..." He confided the Soviet Strategic Plan to the two men. Phase one, 'The Period of Preparation for Peaceful Co-existence', was retrospective and covered the time from the 20th Communist Party Congress of 1956 to the 21st Congress in 1959.

Phase two, 'The Peaceful Co-Existence Struggle' lasted from 1960 to 1972, the year after the 24th Party Congress. The main strategic objectives were to promote disunity in the West and accelerate social fragmentation of the capitalist countries. "In Europe, we exaggerated fears of a renascent Germany and played upon French nationalism to drive a wedge between France and NATO" the General Secretary said. "We used our penetration of European Social Democratic Parties to weaken their ties with the United States and strengthen their willingness to accommodate the Warsaw Pact. By manipulating the trade union movement and student organizations we exacerbated existing causes of social and industrial unrest and created areas of confrontation. We exploited anti-Americanism in Europe in order to undermine America's commitment to Europe's defense. Inside the United States we encouraged isolationism and stirred up internal disorder, focusing the attacks of the radical movement over there on the military and industrial establishments as barriers to peace. Here we received an unexpected bonus from the Vietnam War," he said.

"In the third world, our aims were to destroy 'colonialism', weaken the economies of the old colonial powers and win new allies in the effort to discredit the 'Imperialist powers', led of course by the United States. No one can deny our success in these objectives. The new balance of votes in the United Nations was pivotal. In the Middle East we encouraged Arab nationalism, urged the nationalization of oil, and laid the groundwork for the overthrow of the Arab monarchies and their replacement by progressive governments" the General Secretary confided.

He went on, "The main strategic purpose of phase three, 'The Period of Dynamic Social Change' is to smash the hope of false democracy and bring about the demoralization of the West. Our relationship with the United States is the vital element in this phase. We must get American leaders to doubt their intelligence services. By fostering belief in our policy of friendship and cooperation with America, we will receive the greatest technological assistance from the West, and at the same time convince the capitalist countries that they have little need for military alliances. The erosion of NATO begun in phase two will be completed by the withdrawal of the United States from its commitment to the defense of Europe, and by European hostility to military expenditure, generated by economic recession and fanned by the efforts of the progressive movements."

He did not reveal that they even considered the possibility of dissolving the Soviet Union, but he added, "In phase three, capitalism will suffer an economic crisis that will bring Europe to its knees and stimulate the influence of progressive forces."

"The fourth and final phase of the plan will be the dawn of 'The Global Democratic Peace'. At the start of phase four the US will be isolated from both Europe and the developing countries. We will undermine it by use of external economic weapons, and so create the social and economic conditions for progressive forces to emerge inside that country." Nikolay drank it all in. The General Secretary's plans for him were clearly as large as his own plans for himself. This was *Comrade Pike's* most satisfied moment in life. He was now a man standing where destiny intended him to be. He wished his father could see how he had made it into the inner circle.

The General Secretary explained historical détente: "They think we are surrendering to the capitalists. They don't understand that it gives us a free hand – a free hand to almost all the communist movements in the world- and this is most important."

Emboldened, Nikolay asked for details. Feeling the vodka's warm glow from inside, The General Secretary provided them: "In order to promote a swing to the left within Britain and force the pace of radical change, progressive forces must take over the trade unions and penetrate the Labour Party. First, however, the role of the trade union movement must be changed, so that it becomes accepted as a pillar of government." He added, "we can assist with 'discoveries' of damning information on hostile politicians." He was on a roll and he was all over the place, "International companies, especially those under American ownership must be targeted. When we have forced out management and had "workers' committees" take over their factories, Ford and General Motors will be our trophies."

"If we can impose on the USA the external restraints proposed in our plan, and seriously disrupt the American economy, the working and the lower middle classes will suffer the consequences and they will turn on the society that has failed them. They will be ready for revolution. We must polish up our efforts to recruit high-level agents of influence in the American government, media, and academic elite" – It was then that *Comrade Pike* called The General Secretary "Yuri", and The General Secretary did not bat an eye. *Comrade Cardinal,* on the other hand, could not afford such a dangerous gamble.

Comrade Cardinal read clearly what was going on tonight. Every officer at the field grade or above in the Warsaw Pact knew the broad strokes of The Long-Term Strategic Plan for the Next Ten to Fifteen Years and the Years After.* With so many thousands sharing the secret, it was a certainty that the CIA had heard this plan, though the Soviets made considerable efforts to give the impression that such complicated long-term planning was folly. The Americans seemed to accept that view without much prompting. Regardless, the General Secretary was a master manipulator. He made *Comrade Pike* feel historically important and he sensitized him to what his commander's intent was at the same time, though *Comrade Cardinal* thought the vodka *had* loosened his tongue. As much as they had already accomplished, future accomplishments would now be an accelerating geometric progression.

*See *We Will Bury You- The Soviet Plan for the Subversion of the West by the Highest Ranking Communist Ever to Defect* by Maj. Gen. Jan Sejna (Sidgwick & Jackson, 1982).

2.

PNC CONVENTION
CHARLOTTE,
NORTH CAROLINA
8:10 P.M.
13 SEPTEMBER 2012

The 2012 Progressive National Committee convention prepared to ratify their platform with a voice vote on live television. They had announced their platform on the opening night of the convention and it was the same as in recent years with just a few minor tweaks. The phrase, "One nation under God" had been removed from a platform otherwise consistent with that of the previous convention. It seemed to be time to make the change. Belief in God was a reactionary holdover.

The national press corps was generally sympathetic to President Mallory Winston's agenda and was always hesitant to be overly critical of the first woman president. After all, she did a great job of drawing national attention to the topics of racism and sexism. She had done more to advance gay rights than any other president, she was strong on the environment, and she had even encouraged the United Nations to do more to prevent hate-speech against Muslims. She had shown the courage required to accept the loss of popularity necessary to push through a national healthcare plan, and the only thing keeping her predecessor's stupid decisions from collapsing the economy after the 2008 financial crises were the multi-billion dollar 'stimulus' packages that she fought for.

But, there *were* a couple of mentions of the platform change within her party. It was the fault of a couple of internet bloggers, followed closely by relentless talk radio babble, really. Once there was strong enough interest in the story it had to be mentioned. Fortunately, President Winston's chief of staff, Hillary Barrett moved swiftly. She had arranged for convention speaker, Los Angeles Mayor Dennis Gomez to announce that President Winston had heard about the platform oversight and personally insisted they hold a vote to put it back in.

Addressing the crowd, Mayor Gomez said "All those delegates in favor, say aye…" and there was a shout of "aye". "All those delegates opposed, say no." And there was a thunderous roar of "no".

Mayor Gomez announced, "In the opinion of the…" then he realized he had received a 'no' vote. Feigning uncertainty he said "Let me do that again". He took the votes again and every viewer across the country witnessed the same outcome.

Between this and whatever happened in Benghazi, he knew that announcing a vote against God would cost his party the 2012 elections. Sweating heavily, he stammered, "I am... I guess..." and a female voice came to the rescue. The on screen coordinator, at the side of the stage said, "You gotta let them do what they're gonna do."

Regaining some composure and hoping for the best, Mayor Gomez said again "I'll do that one more time. All those delegates in favor, say aye". There was a shout of aye. "All those delegates opposed, say no." There was a roar of "no".

The Mayor then read off his prompter: "In the opinion of the chair, two-thirds have voted in the affirmative, the motion is adopted and the platform has been amended as shown on the screen". He abruptly turned and stormed off stage before a booing crowd. Damn it, he thought, how could they pack the convention with radicals? Did these people want to win or not?

Watching the event on live-television, President Mallory Winston demanded "What the hell was that?!" The cable networks would be atwitter repeating that loop for the next ten minutes. Hillary Barrett was on speaker and Saleha Said, deputy chief of staff for re-election, sat across from her. Barrett was always decisive and calm. Even as the cable news anchors were still gasping, she said, "We will put out the word to our friends. This is a non-event. The platform inadvertently left out mention of God, you insisted we have a vote to put it back in, and it was voted back in. I'll have our people start calling their contacts now." She clicked off.

President Winston looked at Said and cried, "We're going to lose this whole damn thing over this and Benghazi!"

Saleha Said, an early thirties beauty from Virginia said soothingly, "We can manage this. Hillary will get her people on putting this platform thing to bed, and all you have to do with Benghazi is stay consistent. Stick to the talking points. Muslim protesters objected to the Nakoula Video and one of these protests got out of hand. If you stay away from defensive language, this is an opportunity to caution against slandering Islam."

Winston's people had recently been pushing the slogan "General Motors is alive and Osama bin Laden is dead." She had even gone so far as to say that al Qaeda was "done" in some interviews. The fact that some of the Benghazi attackers had been positively identified as al Qaeda operatives was not something Winston's people felt they could afford to admit. Besides, there were members of other groups represented among the attackers as well- President Winston was convinced that didn't mean much anyway.

Winston continued, albeit more calmly, "There have already been photos of mortar impacts and intact mortar tailfins from the embassy annex in the news" she said referring to a news report one of her advisers told her about. "Obviously rioters don't have mortars with them, only militants executing a planned mission do," Winston thought to herself. Evidence that Benghazi was not a protest, or even a riot, was already in the public domain. Eventually one of the survivors would talk- regardless of her orders.

Said could read the President well though and she knew that the President had been calmed. She said confidently, "You just concentrate on doing what you do best, and leave the rest to us; if the press starts asking real questions about Benghazi we'll have the Attorney General have Nakoula arrested... That won't hold up forever, but it *will* take us through the election".

2.01

AL BALAD STREET
JEDDAH, SAUDI ARABIA
10:00 A.M. 14 JULY 1989

Aliyah's mother held her hand in the backseat of their shiny white Mercedes, while a man she didn't know drove silently. Aliyah was a highly perceptive 14 year old, and even though they both wore black cloaks with hoods and veils that covered everything but their eyes she could easily read her mother's demeanor. She stared at the henna design on the hand that held hers and wondered what was going on. Mother hadn't held her hand in this way since she was a little girl.

For some reason, this day reminded her of the day father had shared a great secret with her. One day, he had walked with her and told her that her Islam studies must advance. He told her that to that point she had studied the Koran as children do, reading about peace and love and personal surrender to Allah. After that day, however, she studied Koranic verses that called for blood and the subjugation of non-believers. She and her father read *Milestones* by Sayyid Qutb together, *Jihad* by Hasan al-Banna and they studied *The Protocols of the Elders of Zion.*

Father had explained the concept of *kitman* to young Aliyah. He told her that it was never permissible to deceive her father, but that subterfuge to advance the will of Allah was necessary. Week after week, they read excerpts from scholars that made similar assertions.

Aliyah knew that her family was different; she knew they were special. Both of her parents had PhDs and were professors. They had moved to Saudi Arabia from Dearborn, Michigan before she was old enough to remember, though she believed her easy fluency in English probably came from that time. She knew that father was a member of an important organization that she was not allowed to speak to anyone about. She knew her older brothers were also members, and she knew that her mother supported their activities. She knew she would have an important role to play one day. Aliyah felt lucky to be a woman serving Allah knowing she had an important duty of her own to carry out.

Aliyah followed in the footsteps of her parents. Her intellect was well above average and everything about this day told her that another piece of this puzzle was going to be revealed to her. She was excited and filled with anticipation, even if she read concern on the part of her mother. That was…unusual. Mother had been distant ever since the day she first bled; ever since she became a woman.

When their mysterious driver eased backward into a parking space, Aliyah felt only a twinge of apprehension. They got out and walked behind him. Aliyah could tell that the familiarity of her mother's demeanor toward him was an act. She wondered why only mother was here and not father.

As they walked, her mother spoke to her quietly. Her tone was uncharacteristically soft. Aliyah felt almost as though she were apologizing; but for what, she could not guess.

"...you must be prepared to live among the infidels..." mother said "...to accomplish all that you have been put on this earth to do." This sounded very final. "...you must be stronger than any man..." Aliyah was beginning to feel fear now. Her mother had never spoken this way before. "...you must be willing to do what others cannot do...you must be able to do what others would not do...for Allah...you must understand that you are his instrument...and what other people are forbidden you are permitted...in *His* service...you must be able to embrace the unimaginable..."

"Enough!" the stranger said tersely, speaking for the first time. He pulled Aliyah's hand from her mother and brought her to the door of a shabby garage a few steps away. Her knees were shaking now and she felt like a little girl. She was not a woman at all. She wanted mother to protect her.

When the man dragged her through the door, mother was no longer with her. The room was dimly lit to her eyes used to the outside sun light. One wall was an aluminum door that could roll up to admit cars. She could make out three middle aged men on a couch. She had to swallow to moisten her dry mouth. Two were balding, one had a destroyed eye and a long Wahhabi style beard.

It wasn't until a moment later that she was able to pick out the form of two nude teen-aged boys in front of her. Over the coming days she was raped by each of them and other visitors repeatedly. Throughout the entire experience she was assured that only martyrdom could save her from her shame. These men knew what they were doing. Aliyah was not their first victim. Their most recent 'trainee' had walked into a Jerusalem pizza shop and detonated 20 pounds of concealed TATP and nails less than one week ago. From this day forward Aliyah would never be the same person. From this day forward Aliyah was...numb. Anything else would be an act.

2.02

KGB SAFE HOUSE

SAINT PETERSBURG, RUSSIA

7:40 P.M. 21 APRIL 1991

"Old friend, it's good to see you" *Comrade Cardinal* said, sipping his vodka.

Nikolay Sludtsev sat across from him looking tense. He sat forward on the couch, glass in hand and untouched by his lips, wearing a tailored Italian suit that appeared as dour as his mood.

A lot had happened recently. General Secretary Gorbachev - feeling the collapsing pressures of a State run economy - had been pushing the concepts of *glasnost*: openness and *perestroika*: restructuring. So far the international press had not seemed to notice that several of his predecessors had used similar campaigns, sometimes with near-identical slogans, to strengthen their positions too, but they *could* wake up at any moment.

The General Secretary of the Communist Party had been dealt the challenging hand of being the man at the helm when the stagnancy of socialism and the economic warfare of President Ronald Reagan had ended the ability of anyone to lay any more tracks in front of the train that was the Soviet economy.

The Russian economy was imploding and legendary investor and philanthropist Nikolay Sludtsev had been one of several prominent individuals asked by U.S. President Richard Winston to serve on Ambassador-At-Large Johnson DeBeers' advisory team visiting the new and independent States emerging from the former Soviet Union. At the moment, however, the only thing Sludtsev cared about was the fact that he could be executed for treason in the United States if his relationship with the KGB were to come to light. The fact that government prosecutors would not want the Sludtsev story to become public knowledge any more than he did did not reassure him. He figured that leverage point would get him a prison sentence rather than death. But prison would be as bad as death as far as he was concerned.

"General Secretary Gorbachev is the only other living person that knows your status", *Comrade Cardinal* lied. Yuri Andropov had died, but no other soul had ever been informed about *Comrade Pike.* On the 9th of February, 1984 the circle of people that knew about Sludtsev's special mission shrunk to two.

"You were insulated from the start. Your work is of the highest importance. The officer that screened you and brought you to Chairman Andropov's attention was told to discontinue pursuing you because we suspected you were loyal to the United States and would likely provide information to the CIA. Since that day you have never been mentioned in any cables or KGB documents."

The American replied, "Mr. Gorbachev will face tremendous pressure. He is disassembling the previous government. He will eventually do what he has to do..."

Comrade Cardinal interrupted, "Nikolay, the General Secretary is not a Композиция from off the street. He is a shrewd man. He rose to General Secretary of the Communist Party of the Soviet Union. Do you believe that he served The Party faithfully every day for the past 60 years in order to one day tear down Soviet Socialism? He hasn't even made such a claim. He said that *perestroika* will be the restructuring of our economy to employ socialism that can make use of creativity to accomplish productivity." He said truthfully. The world simply heard what the world wanted to hear.

"That doesn't mean that he won't be pressured to give us up..." Nikolay said in a tone that sounded uncomfortably close to a whine.

His case officer interrupted him. "Nikolay, *you* are a wise man. You *know* that all crisis carries opportunity. This one is no different." Over the next 48 minutes Sludtsev's friend explained how they had been personally chosen by the General Secretary to be the guardians of international socialism.

With steeled will and a renewed sense of purpose *Comrade Pike* strode to the door. "I have to get going." He was wary from the nearly three hour route he had to run to guarantee he was clean going to the safe house and the rollercoaster of a conversation, but mentally he was electrified by the thought of his new opportunities.

Suddenly he looked pensive and said, "I need to speak with DeBeers, we have a phone conference."

"Don't worry about that buffoon" *Comrade Cardinal* said with disdain. He regarded American bureaucrats as naïve functionaries with no knowledge of world history and little understanding of human behavior.

Sludtsev was looking him in the eye when *Comrade Cardinal* added, "He is one of our *Special Unofficial Contacts*" referencing what he had been told by another KGB officer that had recently been transformed into an SVR officer when the KGB was renamed.

Over the next 30 days the two men undertook their special mission. More than $60 billion dollars disappeared from the dissolving Communist Party of the Soviet Union's accounts. More than $48 billion of it would surreptitiously find its' way into *Comrade Pike*'s network of entities. Over the next year Russia's liquidated State assets became the property of the *oligarchs;* Russia's new "businessmen". The plums ended up under companies in the Magna-Stellar Fund. The Free Community Partnership and its' army of front groups was now the most highly funded disinformation campaign in human history. By far.

2.03

10 DOWNING STREET
LONDON, ENGLAND
7:25 P.M.
16 SEPTEMBER 1992

Prime Minister John Major realized he had been digging his fingers into the soft leather arms of his chair and consciously willed himself to relax. "What bloody well happened?" was the question of the day.

Three clean cut Englishmen in neat suits stood before him taking turns speaking in hopes of providing an answer. His head throbbed and he wished he could wake up and discover this was a dream.

The United Kingdom, had been inflating its' currency supply to allow the government to spend more than it actually had. This, of course, was just standard practice for governments. It was essentially an invisible tax created by printing currency (or electronically doing the same) that elevated spending power for those closest to the seat of power and diluted the value of the pound in the pocket of the man on the street.

While an individual with a £10 note would still have the same note after inflation, it would simply buy less as a portion of its' value was shifted to the newly created notes being spent. The world naturally and unavoidably reacted to an increasing number of pounds pursuing the same amount of goods and services in the marketplace. The practice could be likened to cutting a pizza normally divided into six slices into eight so that the government had two more slices to eat. You would still get the slice you paid for; it would just be smaller.

The United Kingdom had drastically downsized its' military and defense spending after World War II and the dissolution of the British Empire, but socialist policies had become fashionable decades ago. As a result, productivity and economic growth were stifled with well-intended regulation. All-the-while governmental expenditures grew continuously as an ever increasing number of services were promised by those in office and those seeking office.

By 1990, Prime Minister Margaret Thatcher's economic advisor, Alan Walters- the man who had publicly refuted the idea of participating in ill-conceived financial schemes- was long gone. His replacement saw an opportunity to artificially "set" the value of the pound sterling and join the European Exchange Rate Mechanism.

Citizens scarcely noticed. The pound was propped up. Obviously, market forces would catch up- you can't cheat gravity forever- but, that would be on somebody else's watch and it would be their responsibility to work their own magic.

On 16 September 1992, gravity caught up. Several key market players sold a large volume of pounds. When the herd saw the trend, more and more traders began to bail out of their pound holdings. The UK Treasury attempted to fight the tide.

The Prime Minister okayed their emergency mission and they began borrowing aggressively. By mid-day, they realized they couldn't beat the market. They had raised interest rates to 12% and promised to go to 15%. The Treasury spent £27 billion; but gravity took over. Anyone capable of basic addition and subtraction was in a position to see that the pound was being artificially propped up, and when it looked like major players were maneuvering out from under a falling boulder, all market players did the same. No one wanted to be the last man on the hook in this unravelling pyramid scheme.

By the end of the day the U.K. government realized it was out of options. The Treasury gave up its' effort to prop up the pound and was no longer eligible to stay in the European Exchange Rate Mechanism. A national recession followed. As with so many euphemistically named programs, taxpayers created a more blunt name for the ERM. They called it the "Eternal Recession Mechanism".

It was not until after that first day that Mr. Majors was advised that Nikolay Sludtsev's Magna-Stellar Fund had led the panic. Sludtsev had put $10 billion at risk short selling the pound. He made another fortune and safed his resources in less than one day. The United Kingdom faced a very bitter free-market pill to return to health, or a heavier dose of socialism to mask the illness. The man who had given Sludtsev his mission had no idea who would be Prime Minister on this day, but he knew human nature. He knew the choice that would be made, and he knew the choices that would have to be made to sustain the previous choices.

Some men are content to play checkers for their entire lives. Some men choose to play the game of chess. In the days to come, Nikolay Sludtsev experienced great pleasure watching independent Internet *opinionistas* accuse billionaire activist George Soros of his plots.

2.04

K STREET

WASHINGTON, DISTRICT

OF COLUMBIA

5:20 P.M.

12 AUGUST 1994

First Lady Mallory Winston sat behind crossed arms opposite her executive assistant with several staffers arrayed around the table in between them. She required the agent-in–charge of her Secret Service protective detail to wait in the outer lobby, and the other agents were outside standing-by, or more precisely, sitting-by in their black Suburbans. They had been convening for nearly a year in this leased brick office. Ms. Winston had been named by her husband to head-up his Task Force on National Healthcare Reform. This was an unusual move, but she was an experienced attorney, she had a lifetime of political activism experience under her belt, and she had political ambitions of her own. The arrangement put someone very close to President Richard Winston behind the steering wheel of his highest legislative priority and it paid her back with high-level national policy experience she hoped to use as a stepping stone to bigger things.

Healthcare in the United States had begun as it had everywhere. It was a private venture in which individuals paid or traded for the services they wished to obtain. Over the decades, politicians promising ever more to constituents had insinuated government power into medicine. The government funded hospitals, and regulated and approved medical practices. While state run healthcare had proliferated in Europe, Americans had always resisted the rationing of services and stifling of innovation that is requisite to central planning- even when tied to the promise of a 'free lunch' - or in this case, 'free' medical care.

In 1994 it was a stretch to say that medicine in America was still practiced in a free-market, but individuals could purchase the services they wanted, purchase insurance of their choosing - albeit heavily regulated - or simply avail themselves of emergency care that they would receive a bill for after the fact. Laws prevented turning away emergency patients in most cases, so a significant number of individuals received emergency care and never paid for the services they received. The costs were absorbed by the provider and passed on in billing to others. When you paid to put your arm in a cast, you were paying for your cast and you were paying a percentage of someone else's cast that had not paid for the services they received.

Using this fact as justification, President Richard Winston had advocated healthcare reform and had appointed a task force. Mr. Winston wanted a national healthcare system provided by the State. He had written on the subject at different times throughout his career. Regrettably, Americans would never voluntarily swallow the concept of 'socialism' even if promised to be limited to only one segment of the economy. Richard knew, however, how much good could be done if he could achieve his goal. The average American would hardly notice what he lost, but non-emergency medical care could be extended to *every* person in the country. No citizen would be denied 'coverage' because she had a pre-existing ailment. No international visitor would wonder what to do when in an accident while visiting the United States. No illegal immigrant would face a health concern caused by poverty. This policy would do *so* much good... and he could not deny the power it would give him and his political party. Redistributing a little from a few to the many would create far more friends than enemies. He would be a hero and implementation would be the ultimate carrot and stick for any president to wield. He would have billions to send to those who needed it and his people would, of course, be able to get it to them through the hands of friends. Nobody would be able to afford to resist his 'powers of persuasion'.

The U.S. Task Force for Healthcare Reform *had* been controversial. The press had been told that it was a collection of the best and brightest in medicine, collected to advise the President with a proposed course of action to improve the delivery of healthcare for all and reduce costs. Before long, however, there were public complaints about the secretive nature of the task force. It was never disclosed to the public who was on the task force and the minutes of their meetings were never shared. It became increasingly clear that the task force saw its' mission as getting a bill passed for the President, not *learning* anything about medicine or insurance markets.

By mid-1994 several lawsuits had been filed to roll back the secrecy under the Federal Advisory Committee Act. A friendly judge, hesitant to undermine the initiative of another branch of government provided a creative ruling that essentially decided that a President's wife could be considered a government employee rather than a private citizen- allowing the veil of secrecy to be maintained. This maneuvering ultimately undermined the task force's popularity, however.

TV ads paid for by people ranging from medical insurance companies, to doctors associations and individual citizens that wanted free-market solutions instead of socialized medicine proliferated the airwaves. Eventually a lawsuit by a physician's association to find out who was on the task force was upheld, but instead of providing the information, the task force elected to pay a quarter of a million dollars in fines. By August, the proposed bill that everyone was calling "Mallorycare" was dead. Socialized medicine would not extend to America in 1994.

Meanwhile, on K Street, Mallory Winston was walking around the room. The only thing left to do was to pack up and move out. She pressed the panic button on the broach she was wearing and smiled coolly as her Secret Service man burst through the door.

"Bill, Cindy will show you the files I need to keep." Ms. Winston said, gesturing to one of her interns.

"Can you and your men get them together?" she said with two things in mind. This policy initiative had to be revisited one day; it would be good for America. She also admitted to herself, that she had no idea when that opportunity would return.

"Yes, Ma'am" the agent-in-charge said. He had reacted to the alert efficiently, but by now he knew that it was most likely a summons to come carry something.

2.05

AL HILLAH PALACE
BABIL PROVINCE, IRAQ
4:00 P.M. 14 APRIL 1995

Comrade Thorn walked along a concrete pathway overlooking what had been the ancient city of Babylon. He was handed a sun bleached brick. After looking at King Nebuchadnezzar the second's image on it, his host pointed out the images on the bricks in the wall. Nebuchadnezzar bricks had been replaced with bricks bearing the image of Saddam Hussein on each one. That's how power was exercised *Comrade Thorn* thought to himself as the sun beat down and his perspiration flowed freely. History is continuously re-written by whomever holds the stage of the present.

He had graduated the KGB's "Institute" nearly two decades before and had been a case officer for his entire adult life. Of course, these days he was now considered an SVR officer and he worked for Department MS (Measures of Support) rather than Directorate A (Active Measures), but nothing had changed except names. There was less talk of Soviet Socialism in his organization, but the world was still a hostile place. Mother Russia still needed to be protected. Russia had been vulnerable, and the capitalists had brought her to her knees. There was a currency collapse. Crime was rampant and people lined up for scraps of bread. *Comrade Thorn* knew better than anyone that it would be a tough climb if Russia were to claw her way back to strength and he was proud to be a warrior in that fight.

Qusay Hussein walked hand in hand with the man he knew as Andrei. Both men enjoyed the hilltop view from the palace and looked out toward the Euphrates River. Qusay wore a business suit, shirt unbuttoned, with no tie. Hand holding was not something he always did, but he found the Arab custom made foreigners uncomfortable and he preferred having the man he knew as Andrei ill-at-ease. The men had met intermittently for years; Qusay representing the interests of his father, Saddam, the "President" of Iraq and 'Andrei' representing the interests of his agency.

Most recently, Iraq had been suffering under American driven United Nations sanctions. Nearly all overt commerce was embargoed between Iraq and the international community. American President Richard Winston's administration had proposed an oil-for-food program in order to limit the suffering of the people of Iraq, and the unpopularity of being associated with causing it. The United Nations set up the Office of the Iraq Program to administer the undertaking and by 1995 it was well underway.

An escrow type account had been set up. The Iraqi State Oil Marketing Organization (SOMO) created vouchers representing blocks of 1 million to 10 million barrels of oil. SOMO could sell the vouchers to international vendors of its' choosing within a price range set by the U.N. The product was permitted to be shipped from Iraq and the payment went into the escrow account. The account was used to buy a range of food, medicine and other humanitarian type expenses that the U.N. approved.

Qusay, long experienced at the skills necessary for holding power in a Machiavellian world, had been privy to the operations of Iraq's intelligence services. Iraq had compromised and controlled a number of U.N. officials, but like all outlaw regimes and wealthy trans-national criminals, Qusay understood that the KGB, now SVR, owned more people in the U.N. than Iraq did and he suspected maybe even more than everyone else combined. Andrei had boasted to him that Russian disinformation activities had been so successful over the past decades that they now had assets in place in virtually every office of the U.N. happy to undermine the USA for nothing more than occasional "gifts" of cheap gold jewelry purchased with cash from a Walmart a short drive from U.N. headquarters in New York City.

Qusay and *Comrade Thorn* began their oil-for-food initiative by steering the vouchers to friendly individuals and organizations. These collaborators sold the vouchers to parties interested in receiving oil and received a nice, but allowable windfall for playing a role in the transaction.

The Norwegian program representative, Arnstein Wigestrand would resign in 1997. The American representative, Maurice Lorenze, would resign in 1998 and Bernard Cullet, the French representative resigned in 1999. The only remaining oversight was from *Comrade Sid*, the Russian Representative. Russia, China and France successfully blocked the replacement of the absent representatives.

With an SVR officer supervising the U.N. oil-for-food program, Qusay and *Comrade Thorn* no longer had a price-control limit on the voucher exchanges. Iraqi oil was on the world market, the money flowed back to Saddam and the facilitators took a healthy cut.

By the time *Comrade Thorn* stepped back into the immaculate Mercedes Qusay dispatched to shuttle him to Baghdad International Airport the two men had updated their arrangement. As Qusay's security men in suits with short barrel 'Krinkov' style AK-47s stepped out of the car's path Andrei contemplated the report he would be making.

Comrade Thorn would make an enormous sum for some well-placed friends of the Russian government. He knew the resources he brought to Mother Russia would secure his career and provide him the opportunity to become a wealthy man too. Vouchers for 79,800,000 barrels of oil went to the Liberal Democratic Party of Russia. 34,000,000 went to the Peace and Unity Party and many millions more went to other organizations and individuals that needed to be rewarded. Nearly $64 billion of oil was diverted. Nearly half-a-billion dollars went to influential Russians. Most of the rest was laundered through a network of shell companies and fronts.

Comrade Thorn would have been surprised to learn that much of it ended up in the accounts of some of the American Magna-Stellar fund's companies and billionaire Nikolay Sludtsev's philanthropic interest, the Free Community Partnership. In coming years a few slivers of the Iraqi oil-for-food scam would make it into the public domain. While many of the embarrassing details were suppressed, too many existed to hide them all. A $485,000 "consulting fee" was even discovered in a bank account of U.N. Secretary General Kofi Annan's son, Kojo. Of course the oil had already been delivered, the funds had already been disbursed and nobody made much of an effort to suffer the embarrassment of serious investigations.

2.06

WALL STREET
NEW YORK, NEW YORK
11:20 A.M. 14 MAY 1997

Nikolay Sludtsev felt the way that he thought Julius Caesar must have felt at the Battle of Alesia. At some point, Caesar must have known with certainty that his efforts were going to be successful. There had to have been a moment when he saw, before anyone else did, that the Gallic tribes *were* going to be defeated; Celtic dominance from modern day France to northern Italy *was* going to be smashed. The Roman Empire *was* going to expand again and Caesar knew that he was the man who caused it.

This was that moment for Sludtsev. He had just stepped out of the conference room adjacent to his office suite for the Magna-Stellar Fund and spoke into his cell phone. He was repeating the news he had just given the three men sitting around the largely open hand carved Carpathian Elm conference table. The three men were not employees or business allies. They were competitors.

Sludtsev informed them that he had moved the considerable resources of the Magna-Stellar Fund out of the way of the falling Thai baht and Malaysian ringgit. In fact, he had been buying assets within South East Asia for several years, but the baht, like any other modern currency, had vulnerabilities.

All currencies start life tied to something of value, such as gold. This is how trust is earned and people can be convinced to use the currency. Once a population has accepted a currency, it is a standard matter of human psychology that the powerbrokers associated with the production of currencies see opportunities for additional gain. If the currencies are severed from their ties to underlying value, oblivious populations generally don't abandon them immediately, and small, nearly painless manipulations in the money supply are enormously profitable for those close to power.

The major problem is that the imperceptible damages from these small manipulations are cumulative. No matter how large the overall dangers of destroying the value of a currency based on nothing but government promises becomes, there is always one more bureaucrat or friend of the powerful that can justify one more "harvest" for himself. In Caesar's day this was done by bureaucrats literally shaving off the edges of gold and silver coins before sending them back into circulation, today this is done by central banks inflating the money supply. The challenge is that people eventually notice that their coins are shrinking and choose to find other ways or other currencies to trade for what they want. This vulnerability is common to every fiat currency through history.

By January of 1997 Nikolay Sludtsev realized that these vulnerabilities were bubbling close to the surface in the Thai economy. He used $700 million from the Magna-Stellar war chest against the baht. He convinced a competitor that the baht's reckoniong could be at hand and his fund bet $3 billion against the baht.

The Thai government fiercely defended the baht for fears that a devaluation would destroy the balance sheets of the country's banks and corporations. Thai politicians believed the baht was their dairy cow to milk, not Sludtsev's beef cow to slaughter. Thailand's external debt at that time stood at $100 billion. Every Bt1 devaluation would add Bt100 billion to that debt.

By the time Nikolay revealed to the last of the competitive contacts he enjoyed speaking to that the baht was destined to fall, The Thai central bank had fought the currency war until they spent all the country's foreign exchange reserves - more than $30 billion in six months. The battle climaxed on May 14th when Sludtsev's fund and his cohorts bet $10 billion against the baht, trying to destroy the currency peg system and devalue it.

The following day the Thai government cut off the links between offshore and onshore baht markets. Speculators got burnt because they could not get a hold onto the baht to ease their positions. Baht interest rates in the offshore market shot up 3,000 per cent in one day. But Sludtsev's fund was not affected significantly since it had sold the baht short in the forward market, with maturity dates of six months and one year.

The Bank of Thailand hoped to turn the tables on Sludtsev - and hurt him with the creation of the two-tier currency system. But inside the central bank's headquarters, officials were nervous. They knew that they were inching ever closer to the abyss after they had spent all their foreign exchange reserves defending the baht.

Just as with the Bank of England, Sludtsev would not be dissuaded once he joined the fight. Bureaucracy and inefficiency had created lethal vulnerabilities. Just as in the days of kings, politicians and bureaucrats sincerely believed that they had a divine right to spend and manipulate their people's money. They just didn't realize that they didn't have a monopoly on the power to do it. Nobody does. There will always be a bigger fish somewhere and on this day Nikolay Sludtsev proved to the governments of Thailand and Malaysia that he was their Orca. The nominal GDP of the Association of South East Asian Nations fell by $9.2 billion in 1997 and $218.2 billion (31.7%) in 1998. Sludtsev had 'gotten out of the way' of vulnerable falling currencies at the very same time that they received a little push. And the Sludtsev holdings multiplied again.

2.07

EAST HAMPTON AIRPORT
SUFFOLK COUNTY,
NEW YORK
11:50 A.M.
31 DECEMBER 1999

Nikolay Sludtsev was helped through the sliding door of a Sikorsky S-76 as the blades continued to turn. The down draft whipped his naturally wavy grey hair around in a way that he thought might be pleasant if not for the damned noise and smell of jet fuel being burned. Stepping through the warm blast, he remembered noticing how pilots seemed to love the smell. Fools.

He moved down the white fuselage seeing but not noticing the aircraft's November number silhouetted in a block of royal blue. His mind was elsewhere. He was preoccupied with the deal he was in the middle of making. This was what he lived for. A well maintained female assistant held the glass door to the small Fixed Base Operator (FBO) building he was approaching.

His mind was anticipating the snags that would be arising in his latest venture and plotting their solutions as he walked through a wooden interior door to the FBO's private VIP holding room ambitiously labelled "Premiere's Suite". He sank into a plush leather couch and motioned for what's-her-name to place his hand-crafted galuchat organizer on the small table in front of him.

The door was closed and locked and he took one last scan of her body as he opened the organizer. Her thighs were imperfectly thick, but tight. Her ass was beautiful and her abdomen did not show evidence of excess body fat. Her face was enjoyable without being memorable.

He had come inside as additional travelling luggage was being loaded aboard his Dassault Falcon 900. He needed to call Franco and ask if she was under contract for "entertainment". He could use a blowjob, and even with her imperfections, or perhaps, *because* of her imperfections and her sexy scent, he could really picture enjoying the fucking of her face.

"Please give me a minute…", he said wanting privacy to find out if she was covered under one of his non-disclosure agreements.

He watched her ass as she paraded toward the door. He was confident from the way she invited his attention that she was aware of the lavish compensatory bonuses provided to women in his organizations that pleased him… And out of the corner of his eye, he saw something on the large Panasonic TV opposite him that made him feel as if he were stabbed in the heart.

Comrade Cardinal was on the cable news network that the television was tuned to. Sludtsev's blood stopped flowing. Where the hell was the remote control?! He needed volume. He needed to hear what was going on.

After a quick scramble that seemed to last forever, Nikolay hit the volume-up arrow and broke through the silence. Wearing a dark charcoal suit, an off-white shirt and golden tie with a navy blue pattern, the man Nikolay had known as John Gardner was seated in front of a Christmas tree. He was flanked by the white, blue, and red tri-color flag of Russia on his right and the flag of the President of the Russian Federation featuring the two-headed eagle on his left.

He was addressing the camera; the caption on the bottom of the screen translated…

Dear friends… Today, on the New Year's Eve… I… just like you… together with my relatives and friends… planned to hear the greetings from the President of Russia… Boris Nikolaevich Yeltsin… but it turned out otherwise… today, on December 31, 1999… the first President of Russia decided to resign… He asked me to address the country… Dear citizens of Russia! Dear compatriots! Today, I received upon myself, the duty of the country's head… In three months the elections of the President of Russia will be held… I want to draw your attention to the fact that there will not be a minute of leadership vacuum in the country. There was none, and will be none! I want to warn that any attempts to go beyond the Russian law, beyond the Constitution of Russia, will be stopped on the vine. Freedom of speech. Freedom of conscience. Freedom of mass media. Property rights...these basic principles of the civilized society will be safe under the protection of the state. Military forces, federal border guard service and the law enforcement bodies carry out their work as usual. The state stood and will continue standing as the guarantee of the safety of each of our citizens. In making his decision to transfer the power, the president was acting in full accordance with the country's constitution...only after some period of time can one understand how much this man did for Russia...although one thing is clear already today... The fact that Russia chose the path of democracy and reforms and did not divert from this path and was able to position itself as a strong and independent state- there is his great contribution. I want to wish the first President of Russia, Boris Nikolaevich Yeltsin, health and happiness. New Year is the most bright, kind, and beloved holiday in Russia. As we know, New Year is the time when dreams come true. As for such... unusual New Year, it is even more true! All good and all kind that you hope for will surely come true! Dear friends, only a few seconds... left until the new 2000 year. Let's smile to our dear family members. Let's wish each other warmness, happiness, and love. Let's raise our glasses for the new age of Russia, and for global democratic peace. For love and peace in each of our houses...for the health of our parents and children. Happy New Year! Happy new century!

"Oh my God," Sludtsev thought to himself. His head was swimming. His heart was racing. What did this mean?

Calming himself, Nikolay began reasoning things out... first of all, if *Comrade Cardinal* was now president, his own status was logically *more* secure, *not* at greater risk. Good. Second, how did Gardner pull this off? He had obviously been connected at the top, but this was still shocking. But was it bad? Where did Gardner's funding and support come from? Sludtsev knew that some of the Communist Party money and all of the laundered UN oil-for-food money went where *Comrade Cardinal* had directed, *not* into operations. But that was no surprise. The comrade and his higher-ups would want 'retirement' funds of their own. None the less, this helped Sludtsev prepare to ask himself the big question. The question that he always believed was the reason he was a winner when so many others were los-ers. *Where is the opportunity in this?*

Sludtsev began to feel the warm familiar feeling of excitement. *Comrade Cardinal* had mentioned an opening. He mentioned an election in three months' time. Nikolay didn't know who was backing the man or how big their war chest was, but the one thing he had learned from playing with politicians the world over was that none of them was ever confident that they had enough. No matter how well financed Gardner was, his backers could not have the resources Sludtsev had. They certainly couldn't have as mature a network of international activist groups as he controlled with the Free Community Partnership. In fact the commercial entities they used to liquidate Soviet assets were still largely intact he was sure. Sludtsev was confident he could win Gardner's election.

And then Nikolay began to glow. *He* was on a quest to amass the wealth and power that would prove he was a winner… *the* winner… *and* allow him to remake the world as a better place…as he saw it. But what about Gardner? Gardner never batted an eye when communism was denounced around the world. He now understood with clarity that Gardner's dream was power…and as is common with all of the world's socialists, Soviet Socialism was merely the tool he had been using to acquire it. Sludtsev grinned. He could deliver Gardner what he wanted, and in the process, the student would become the master.

Gardner was no longer *his* case officer. After today, Gardner would be Sludtsev's agent. In fact, why was he even calling him Gardner anymore? What did the television call him? Putin… Vladimir Putin?

Sludtsev picked up his mobile phone and pressed the green button. "Franco…have the flight crew file a new plan immediately. We're going to Moscow."

2.08

SCHWARZMAN BUILDING NEW YORK PUBLIC LIBRARY, NEW YORK
11:50 A.M.
11 SEPTEMBER 2000

FBI Special Agent Ryan Leary of the Counter-Intelligence Division sat staring without expression at the man across the table from him. Leary was thought of as "old school" by the agents under his supervision. He was a no-nonsense guy nearing the end of a long, successful career. He didn't have time to be jerked around and he was never more than a few seconds away from saying so.

On the other side of the table sat a chubby middle-aged man with blonde hair thinning at the right-handed part. They had been talking in a private study cubicle off the Rose room for less than 10 minutes. The chubby man, wearing a striped shirt and blazer, pulled his tie, loosening it slightly before speaking again. Sergei had spent weeks planning this meeting. He didn't choose this site because he liked the high ceilings, brass lamps and grand chandeliers. He picked it because he could afford to disappear from his office to visit this library for a little while. He picked it because he knew it would make the work of the surveillance detection team Leary would have brought with him easier. He picked it because he had a very good library route for detecting surveillance that he had personally constructed to get to this meeting. And despite standing orders, he had not shared that route's existence with his co-workers.

Those co-workers just happened to be Russian SVR officers. Sergei had been a career KGB officer. Now he was an SVR colonel. *Now* he was discussing defecting to the United States.

Leary looked the man in the eyes and said, "...we have the ability to bring your wife and daughter out too if we come to an agreement..."

Leary would have been a great poker player if he had patience for games. His demeanor gave nothing away, but internally he was a child jumping up and down.

The FBI's Counter Intelligence Division had received a cryptic message. A senior SVR officer was supposedly ready to defect. Leary was the man tasked with meeting the proposed defector. Leary would be the first to assess whether the individual setting up the meeting was a dangle - a phony defector orchestrated by the opposition to provide misleading information - or *possibly* the real thing.

The small number of senior FBI CI agents that were aware of the unfolding caper had composed a list of individuals they thought could be the possible defector. It had to be someone in New York. It had to be a supervisor. There were nine names, some simply billets, on the list, but Sergei was the highest hope. He would have access to a treasure trove of information. He would have access to everything the Russians were doing in New York. Even more importantly, he would provide the best look yet into the new world of the SVR... surely things were different from the KGB days.

"What else can you bring?" Leary asked evenly.

Sergei had known this was the most important question to the FBI and he had memorized a list of what he could provide his new friends. Sergei saw himself as a man that had served his motherland as best he could. He had become a KGB officer because that was an avenue open to him through family connections. His father had been an NKVD officer and had survived Stalin's paranoia inspired purges to become a KGB officer.

'Upward mobility' was not something that people had any concept of under Soviet Socialism. Sergei knew he was lucky to have a shot at a privileged life. He always believed he was doing the right thing by serving his countrymen to the best of his ability, but over time he had become disillusioned. He saw the corrupting influence of coercive governmental power everywhere. It was human nature he now realized. The ruling elite was not endowed with greater wisdom than anyone else was, nor were they immune from the natural pressures to wield their power for the benefit of themselves and their closest personal allies. Sergei had come to believe that any state that authorized the government to use deception, coercive powers and manipulation against her own citizens was no different from a medieval monarchy.

The current state of affairs was the final straw. At the same time that Sergei began to admit to himself that he was disenchanted with Soviet Socialism it seemed that society was doing the same. There had been a great upheaval. There had been the predictable collapse of currency that inevitably follows the gluttonous spending of unaccountable bureaucrats who spend other people's money. There had been public demonstrations. And there seemed to be a general feeling that even a Stalin style genocide could not reverse the tide.

Premier Gorbachev, the man left standing at the helm of Soviet Socialism had been a lifelong Communist Party man. Sergei had no doubt his "reforms" would be the minimum he could get away with and retain power. The man had written advocating a "*Marxist* society of free people" in his own book for heaven's sake. Sergei anticipated that this façade of freedom would not survive long. He was right.

Vladimir Putin ended up holding the reins of power and corruption flourished. The wealth of the state that had been the spoils of enslaving a society had disappeared. Physical assets were now 'privately' owned by men well positioned to receive the largesse of government bureaucrats still empowered to direct the economy. Friends of Putin were the new oligarchs.

Senior officials could steal anything not tied down and get away with it so long as the most elite were taken care of. The KGB no longer existed to protect the mother-land and bring down the Main Enemy (the capitalist United States), it had turned into the SVR. It was the same men, with the same capabilities, now dedicated to enriching themselves while paying residual tribute to those in power *and*, it appeared, bringing down the Main Target. The USAs renaming was barely percep-tible. The Russian government was rotten from the top down. It was as if the allies had put Gestapo officers in charge of the "de-Nazification" of the German gov-ernment following the Second World War. Sergei did not want his daughter growing up in such a circus of corruption.

"I can provide our U.N. assets..." Sergei said. This was Sergei's main prize for the Americans if they were willing to help his family. It was transparent to anyone that had ever watched the nightly news that the United Nations seemed to pride itself on biting the hand that fed it; pushing a ridiculous paradigm of equality of legitimacy between the actions of Americans and the actions of tin pot dictators and global thugs that coerced and killed their own people.

Leary was nonplussed. It was taken as an obvious truism among intelligence officers and analysts that quite a few agents of influence had been insinuated into the United Nations to hamstring the United States with asinine policies that could not be taken seriously but for the fact that more colorful news generally pushed them out of the headlines. Leary was wary of threads that would obviously be highly-charged politically. He wasn't sympathetic to U.N. nonsense any more than any other American, but he understood that the political masters that the FBI's director answered to were generally uninterested in confronting U.N. corruption. Besides, he was confident the FBI had a decent handle on the 20 or so foreign intelligence agents in New York that were working for the U.N.

When Sergei calmly stated "…these are 1,211 individuals who both insinuate SVR drafted language into U.N. policies to undermine the United States and report to Russia anything they believe will be of interest to their handlers…" Leary's face froze on Sergei. Leary's heart raced. He wondered if 1,211 U.N. employees were Russian assets, how many were working for the Chinese, North Korea, Iran and every other hostile government and anti-American militant group?

Sergei went on to say, "…you must understand… the KGB's disinformation campaigns have been successful for many decades. Men and women sent to represent their countries with the U.N. show up with strong anti-American leanings. Most people couldn't be bothered to study world history or search out facts that go beyond the superficiality of the evening news. We have run agents from the secretary-general level on down. Many of them are paid with nothing more than scraps of cheap gold jewelry from the Walmart in Secaucus…"

Leary was reeling. If Sergei could pass a polygraph, the FBI would need to do whatever was necessary to bring him in. His mind was already contemplating the wording that would be necessary in his report to allow the FBI to work with this SVR colonel without spooking the higher-ups with the daunting political ramifications.

After Sergei's second meeting with the FBI, *Comrade Jean-* the SVR Chief of Station, New York- was offered the most generous resettlement package that had ever been extended to an SVR officer. He gratefully accepted it.

2.09

UNITED AIRLINES FLIGHT 93 SHANKSVILLE, PENNSYLVANIA 9:25 A.M. 11 SEPTEMBER 2001

On a clear September morning, United Airlines flight 93 was levelled off and headed west. The Boeing 757 had bounced through some minor turbulence, but was cruising smoothly. The flight was only about half full so 26 year old Ziad Jarrah was able to stretch out comfortably. Jarrah was clean cut, with short hair and a fresh shave. He drained the plastic water cup the stewardess had given him and placed it behind the elasticized band in the seatback in front of him. He looked calm, but his heart was racing.

Saeed al-Ghamdi, Ahmed al-Nami and Ahmed al-Haznawi strut purposefully past Jarrah's row. He had known these three Saudis for some time now, and he knew this was going to be the defining moment of his life. They were brothers. Just as brothers squabble, bicker and look out for each other, they had done the same. They annoyed him and he loved them at the same time. Most importantly; he knew they were right. They had long discussions, late into the night on more than a few occasions about the writings of Sayyid Qutb and others. Jarrah had a duty to serve Allah, and his brothers prevented him from being distracted from it.

Ziad looked around and noticed one other passenger take notice of the procession, but no others. Suddenly there was a loud banging from the cockpit cabin. The door had been latched and the two Ahmeds were battering it with one of the aluminum food canisters from the forward galley. Al-Ghamdi was covering their backs brandishing a screw driver. He gestured aggressively at any passenger that might have the courage to make eye contact.

The thin door's latch gave way on the second or third hit and he knew this was the moment of truth. His brothers didn't believe it, but he had heard that some small number of pilots kept pistols on the flight deck. He knew if that was true on this flight, his brothers were dead and this mission was over.

When Ziad heard screams in the cockpit rather than gunshots, he knew they would succeed. The warmth of his girlfriend's body, and the love of his family sadly flashed through his mind, but this was his duty and there was no changing it now. Al-Ghamdi was out of sight in the cockpit and the two Ahmeds were wielding razor utility knives like the ones used to cut carpet. They were herding passengers and stewardesses toward the rear of the cabin.

As soon as they passed Ziad he got up and walked to the cockpit. A bloody, pale, dead looking stewardess lay at the threshold and two pilots lay on the floor, breathing heavily, moaning, and clutching their wounds but offering no more resistance.

Almost immediately after climbing into the left seat, Ziad could see that the pilot had placed the 757s autopilot on. Ziad was a private pilot – he was a pilot of a small single engine, propeller driven Cessna aircraft - but he had just enough time in 757 simulators to know what he needed for this mission.

Ziad punched "Direct To" and "KDCA" and "Enter" into the Flight Management System. He watched the digital icon representing his aircraft start a turn toward Reagan National Airport as he felt the aircraft begin to bank to the east. He keyed the microphone for the transmission he had practiced so many times in his head. "Ladies and gentlemen: this is the captain. Please sit down and keep remaining seated… We have a bomb on board… So sit…" is what came out of his mouth.

One of the pilots on the floor continued struggling and making noise. That was to be expected. What was not to be expected was the struggle he heard from his brothers outside the cockpit. There was shouting and he could hear scuffling at the cockpit door. Someone was fighting his brothers and they were being pressed back to the cockpit. Jarrah scanned his stainless steel watch forgetting there was a clock on the instrument panel. The other planes would have hit their targets by now. If they hadn't been delayed on the runway he would have already flown his 757 into the U.S. Capitol Building and the infidels could cower before their TVs watching the flames burn high.

Saeed, the fool that insisted that he was also a pilot whenever the mission was discussed, stuck his head through the door. "They're all fighting back", he shouted… "Do something!" The hijackers were discovering that several of the passengers had been communicating with the outside world on cell phones. The brother's deception that they were landing to negotiate was not being believed. Ziad used the rudder pedals to skid the aircraft left and right, but he could hear the angry mob recovering and pressing on.

"Get to the cockpit! If we don't, we'll die…" The noise coming from the cabin was terrifying, the mission was completely out of hand. Ziad began jockeying the control yoke violently forward than back. Flailing people went weightlessly to the ceiling and crashing to the floor in the repeated buffeting. "Is that it? Shall we finish it off?" Ziad asked wanting an answer from someone other than Saeed. One of the Ahmeds shouted back, "No, not yet. When they all come, we finish it off."

Ziad heard a passenger yell "Roll it!" and then he felt the cockpit door shuddering. He asked Saeed in a meek voice, "Is that it? I mean…shall we put it down?" and his brother replied, "Yes, pull it down."

Ziad mouthed "Allahu Akhbar" to himself and pushed the aircraft into an unrecoverable banking dive. The altimeter ticked down rapidly and he lost consciousness as the metal buckle of a seatbelt wrapped around a passenger's fist impacted the side of his head. Ziad Jarrah failed in his misson.

On September 11th, 2001, 19 soldiers came to the end of their earthly journey. Each man had been moved to action after reading *The Protocols of the Elders of Zion*, and the writings of Sayyid Qutb, Hasan al-Banna and others. Unlike the weak, they did not fear confrontation. They did not seek the expulsion of Western influence from Islamic lands, the rebirth of a modern caliphate and the dominance of shariah through activism, subversion and manipulation.

They were warriors. They followed one of the *militant* branches of Islamic supremacism. They had thrown in with Osama bin Laden and Ayman al Zawahiri and their goal was to turn jihad into a dynamic war in which every Muslim had to choose a side: infidels or brother Muslims. This was the greatest step of a campaign intended to provoke the United States into bankrupting itself.

2.10

CAPITOL HILL
WASHINGTON,
DISTRICT OF COLUMBIA
5:45 P.M.
6 NOVEMBER 2002

Jim Blaine approached the door to his office in the Capitol building feeling buoyant. He had been working tirelessly on a key piece of legislation for months. Today was the culmination of that effort. The fact that the press crowded him as he walked was recognition of the significance of this undertaking.

Senator Blaine was a likable man. He often came across as a grandfather-type figure. At moments like these, he always reflected on the journey. It had certainly been a long, winding road.

Born in the Panama Canal Zone, he and his mom grew accustomed to moving every few years. That was just the way the navy needed things to be, and dad was an up and coming young officer. In fact, dad, like grand dad had risen up the chain to become an admiral.

Jim followed the example he had been given. He graduated from the Naval Academy in 1958 with the kind of unimpressive academic record that is common to the people who are most effective in the real world. He graduated flight school in Pensacola and went to 'the fleet' flying A-4 Skyhawks. He was the kind of pilot that made an ace in World War II; average academics, a couple of counselings for breaking rules or "recklessness", but a honed skill based on pushing the limits. In the 1960s the US military was discouraging this kind of independent thought in its' officer corps, but it hadn't yet eliminated it.

In 1967 Jim's pushing of life's limits resulted in a parachute ride from a burning A-4. He had skillfully evaded a first volley of surface-to-air missiles fired up by a ground based battery outside Hanoi, but as he rolled away with no more altitude to trade, he rolled into the proximity burst of another SA-2 fired by a cunning Chinese major who had already shot down nine US aircraft while leading a team of advisors operating one of North Vietnam's hundreds of missile sites. Jim nursed the crippled jet to the coast before it burst into flames and he had to eject.

North Vietnamese fisherman pulled him from the sea with two broken arms and a broken leg. They turned him over to an angry crowd on shore that smashed a shoulder with the butt of an SKS and bayoneted him. Soldiers of the North Vietnamese Army took him to the Hỏa Lò Prison.

Jim spent more than five years in captivity. He spent a couple of years- when totaled- in solitary confinement and suffered beatings, food and sleep deprivation as well as being hung from ropes dislocating his shoulders. Jim made the communists fight for every bit of information they extracted from him then made them start over again when they tried to confirm it later. Fellow prisoners said he never betrayed a confidence. By every measure, Jim was a heroic American.

In the early 1980s Jim resigned his commission and was elected to congress. After a relatively short time he was successfully elected to the senate.

Jim Blaine was proud of his record as a senator. He had introduced legislation designed to thwart international oppressors and help individual Americans too many times to count throughout his career. Most recently, he had been working on an initiative to reform campaign contributions. His office had received hundreds of calls, letters and faxes complaining about the sleaziness of campaign financing in American politics, and he had listened. They were right. Corruption was a problem and holes in the system provided quite a few potential avenues for the unscrupulous to take advantage of.

Jim and his staff had taken a close look at the problem and he was happy to discover a kindred spirit in Dean Weinstein, a colleague from "across the aisle". Weinstein - even though a member of the other political party - had had his people looking into the same problem for quite some time. They both agreed on a number of key ideas.

Ultimately the pair introduced a bill commonly called "Blaine-Weinstein". A lot of the grunt work of writing had been done by the people at the Institute for Fair Government, but the key points were these:

- It prohibited national political party committees from raising or spending any funds not subject to federal limits (even for state and local races or issue discussion).

- It prohibited "electioneering communications", broadcast ads that name a federal candidate, within 30 days of a primary or caucus or 60 days of a general election, and prohibited any such ad paid for by a corporation (including non-profit issue organizations) or paid for by an unincorporated entity using any corporate general treasury funds.

Jim Blaine and Dean Weinstein had tackled the problems of "soft money" coming into campaigns and the disproportionate power of issue advocacy ads. In short, both men could take pride in creating some serious hurdles to those who would attempt to buy influence in America's elections.

Both men had been working on this for months. They had successfully introduced the bill, and gotten it passed. On the 6th of November the sister bill that they had had to shepherd through the congressional process with the help of some likeminded congressmen, had come to the floor. Only by being voted into law in the congress also would Blaine-Weinstein become enforceable law for America.

At 5:45 p.m., Jim Blaine was returning to his office after having spent the better part of the day speaking on and off camera in support of his bill. He was tired, but he was excited. He had been successful. Blaine-Weinstein was law. And as he passed through his crowded office door to the celebrations of his staff inside, he felt justifiable satisfaction.

Neither Jim Blaine nor Dean Weinstein would ever know that each phone call their respective offices had received demanding campaign finance reform had come from individuals affiliated with one of six activist groups sponsored by the Free Community Partnership. Neither men would ever realize that the wording of the Institute for Fair Government's writing had not been designed to cut off money for influence in Washington. It was crafted to cut off *other people's* money for influence. Once implemented, the Free Community Partnership and its army of proxies and front groups - the Institute for Fair Government being one - would be the singularly most powerful influence on American politics. After the 6th of November, 2002, the value of Nikolay Sludtsev's political dollars would be magnified. His money was now going to have a whole lot less competition.

2.11

WILSON DRIVE

ANNANDALE, VIRGINIA

2:25 A.M.

29 AUGUST 2004

Special Agent Donald Jackson of the FBI's Washington Field Office SWAT team stood on a reinforced running board on the side of a navy blue Chevy Suburban gripping handholds disguised as a roof rack. This was the part of the job he lived for. As one of a small number of black agents on the Washington SWAT team, he took pride in spearheading important missions. He had been on the team for less than a year.

On this night, Don was in the number two position on the running boards; that is, he was at the front, right of the vehicle. Several other agents also in green Nomex flight suits, ballistic helmets and body armor filled out the other positions. Whereas each other agent had a short barrel M4 with an EoTech sight and PEQ infrared aiming device hanging in front of them, Don had only his holstered 1911 style .45 with Surefire light in the Safariland holster on his leg. He had a Kevlar shield with steps built into the back of it strapped to his back.

The agents had met up at a covered parking garage less than a mile from the target, leaving their individual cars and taking their pre-briefed positions in their respective assault vehicles. Don loved the feeling of the wind in his face and readied himself for his role in this mission. Because the suburban neighborhood had so much ambient light from street lights, the agents all left their NVGs flipped up on their helmets. He recognized the house they were hitting as the driver smoothly pushed the Chevy from one street in between houses toward the 'black' side of their target. The vehicle dipped its' nose as it came to a swift, but non-sliding stop on wet grass.

Don stepped off and flung the ballistic shield off his back and onto his arm as his legs pumped the rest of the distance to the house. If they made contact now, he would be dependent on Rick Davis, his cover man, to do the shooting. Don stopped short of the "1-1" window, the first floor farthest window to the left on the 'green' side of the black-green corner of the home.

He deliberately placed the shield as a ramp from the ground up to the low window sill with the step side up. He stood to the side and drew his .45 without sweeping his team mates who were fulfilling their own tasks. He heard multiple explosions from the 'red' side of the building as teammates detonated a series of flashbangs in an attempt to draw attention away from where they planned to enter. As quickly as Don stepped aside and the flashbangs erupted, another teammate in green took one slash at the window, clearing it from top to bottom with a steel 'hooligan tool'; breaking all the glass panes, destroying the horizontal wooden window divider and pulling out a long swath of curtain fabric that he snagged with the tooth on the end of the device.

Two agents quickly jogged up the ladder and dropped into the room clearing corners with the Surefire lights on their rifles and sweeping the room, meeting in the middle. "Clear" the first said. "Clear" the second echoed and they moved up to the bed room door that led deeper into the house requesting "support" over the boom microphone of an encrypted Motorolla radio. Don knew the room was under control and his teammates were ready to be joined to begin sequentially clearing the rest of the house. When he entered, he could see a sliver of another room where the light was on and a TV cable news channel spewed information about an Environmental Protection Agency report on 'fracking'. Hydraulic fracturing was an American innovation in oil and gas production that put vast quantities of previously inaccessible energy within reach. In fact, combined with some other initiatives, it made North American energy independence possible. The EPA report didn't tie any negative data that was scientifically valid to the practice, but the agency seemed somewhat antagonistic to the idea. Don had seen the same segment earlier. Apparently the suspects watched the same cable news network that the Washington Field Office kept on.

A few days earlier, a police officer in Maryland had witnessed a woman in a colored hijab videotaping the suspension cables and support structures of the Chesapeake Bay Bridge from the back of a minivan. Apparently not having read her agency's policy on 'profiling' too closely, the officer observed the van until it changed lanes without signaling as is required by state statute.

Once off the bridge she hit her flashing lights, conducted a traffic stop and approached with caution. Ismail Elbarasse was behind the wheel. Ismail had an outstanding warrant from a fundraising case for the terrorist group HAMAS. Ismail was detained and FBI agents got a search warrant authorizing them to search his Annandale home.

Because the case was terrorism related, the agents were able to get a 'no-knock' warrant. They served the warrant when they hoped any residents would be asleep in order to mitigate the risks involved with confronting criminals within small arms range of neighbors. HAMAS had been involved in suicide bombings, so grabbing the suspects while they slept was preferred. Because Islamic terrorists had a history of employing explosive booby traps, the SWAT team avoided all the exterior doors and moved with extreme caution.

Nobody was home. Specialists eventually stated that they believed that no explosives were present. After daybreak an evidence team moved in to do comprehensive 'site exploitation'.

Special Agent Nina Saxena made an interesting discovery in the basement. It wasn't the FBIs cutting edge equipment that detected the anomaly. The 27 year old was pleased to point out that the basement was shorter than the rooms above it. Agents discovered a false wall.

Behind the wall, Nina discovered 84 cardboard banker boxes full of documents. It was an archive. One of the documents was entitled "An Explanatory Memorandum: On the General Strategic Goal for the Group in North America".*

The Memo, written in Arabic, explained, "The process of settlement is a 'Civilization- Jihadist Process' with all the word means. The Brotherhood must understand that their work in America is a kind of grand jihad in eliminating and destroying the Western civilization from within and 'sabotaging' its miserable house by their hands and the hands of the believers so that it is eliminated and Allah's religion is made victorious over all other religions." It named 29 of the most influential American Islamic activist groups as "A list of our organizations and the organizations of our friends." When Jackson got word of what they had uncovered, he wondered what "The Brotherhood" was. He made a mental note to do some research...

*See *An Explanatory Memorandum: On the General Strategic Goal for the Group in North America* by Mohamed Akram (Center for Security Policy, 2013).

2.12

MINISTRY OF STATE SECURITY BEIJING, PEOPLE'S REPUBLIC OF CHINA 3:35 P.M. 19 AUGUST 2008

Major General Chiang took a sip of water from his glass and placed the glass back on the dark wooden table. He looked around the room at the collection of People's Liberation Army Officers and the assortment of Communist Party Central Committee members as he listened to the colonel's briefing drone on.

"The Americans have essentially lost $13 trillion in a matter of weeks. It began with the oil run-up of 2007–2008. Prices spiked from approximately fifty US dollars per barrel to 150 dollars. This helped to pierce their government's real estate and derivatives bubbles."

"Please explain these 'bubbles'"… one of the Committee members interrupted.

The colonel respectfully explained that American presidents and politicians attempting to curry favor with voters had increasingly encouraged American banks to provide home loans to a wider and wider segment of the population; to include those who couldn't afford paying for them.

"I don't understand" the Committee member said, "I thought the United States government did not interfere in their markets." He didn't add that he understood this to be an imperfect, but unbeatably efficient model for enterprise; it just didn't lend itself very well to controlling a population.

"No", the colonel responded, "You are correct, of course, regarding the origin of the American model, but the American government regularly intervenes in private transactions and very few are unaffected by political policy today…In fact, American politicians committed the US government to underwriting these… questionable… loans. That is why the banks were eager to fulfill them. They would make money whether the borrower repaid them or not…the 'derivatives' were packages of these loans batched together and sold from a first group of cut throat 'capitalists' to a second group that had not yet figured out their lack of worth."

The colonel explained that when the price of a commodity triples, there are usually winners and losers in capitalist markets. The run-up of oil prices, however, hurt nearly all Americans. The beneficiaries were the major oil-producing countries. In late 2007, while oil prices were rising, massive 'bear raids' targeted several of America's largest financial institutions.

The colonel responded to another question, "A bear raid is a manipulation of a target company's stock price. It is illegal under most nation's laws. The purpose can be the raider's profit, but it can also be something else. Citigroup was hit by short selling in November. American analysts who studied the transactions later concluded that this had been a bear raid."

The colonel stated that the New England Complex Systems Institute (NECSI) retraced events to show that at a critical point in the financial crisis, the stock of Citigroup was attacked by traders selling borrowed stock (short-selling) which appears to have motivated others to sell in panic.

The subsequent price drop enabled the attackers to buy the stock back at a much lower price.

Through its analysis of stock market data not generally available to the public, namely the borrowing of shares, NECSI reconstructed the chain of events. The NECSI analysts estimated that the odds of this kind of trading activity's taking place without deliberate coordination were infinitesimally remote; one said, "When 100 million shares are borrowed on a single day and then returned on a single day, the evidence that this is a concerted action is hard to refute. The likelihood of such an event happening by coincidence is one in a trillion."

The colonel briefed that a few months later, in March 2008, Bear Stearns, America's fifth largest investment bank, was targeted. He cited open-source intelligence from *Rolling Stone magazine saying* the Bear Stearns bankruptcy included an unnamed person making "one of the craziest bets Wall Street has ever seen. The mystery figure spent $1.7 million on a series of options, gambling that shares in the venerable investment bank Bear Stearns would lose more than half their value in nine days or less. It was madness." The next day, Bear Stearns collapsed. The $1.7 million investment was suddenly worth $270 million. It was, according to *Rolling Stone*, "one of the most blatant cases of stock manipulation in Wall Street history." The US government failed to trace it and apparently tried to deny that they were attacked hoping to avoid panic.

A committee member named Li fired an interrupting question at General Wang... "You had nothing to do with this?" General Wang was notorious for his lack of subtlety. He had openly talked about using Chinese held American debt to collapse the remaining vestiges of capitalist systems around the world. He had even written publicly that China should "gather courage" and do this now. China would suffer since America could not repay this debt, but China would be left as the dominant power.

Without emotion or any hint of intimidation, the general replied, "No, sir...We all know that the Putin regime of Russia has been making plans consistent with these attacks, and we know that Mr. Putin's country invited us to join them." He said referring to what he understood were Russia's attacks on Fannie Mae and

Freddie Mac, the government-sponsored entities at the heart of the U.S. mortgage crisis. They had come under attack from short-sellers who recognized their lack of worth. Their stock plunged.

In September, the tactic was repeated. The first target was Lehman Brothers, which experienced a massive spike in short selling. More than one-fifth of trades in Lehman on September 17 were failed trades, a sign of short selling. Lehman's collapse led to the collapses of Merrill Lynch, Washington Mutual, Citigroup, Bank of America, and even Goldman Sachs. AIG was soon on the brink. Over half a trillion dollars had disappeared from U.S. money market accounts. The stock market dropped more than 50 percent - the worst decline since the Great Depression.

"Nobody here today had a hand in these acts?" another committee member asked. He looked around the room at silent and stern faces. America had gaping vulnerabilities. The People's Republic of China had thrown out Chiang Kai-Shek and America's mercenaries at the end of World War II. The People's Liberation Army had deployed hundreds of thousands of troops to Korea to fight the Americans when they were in danger of defeating North Korea in 1950 and they had deployed thousands of pilots, surface-to-air missile operators and advisors to North Vietnam in the 1960s and 1970s enabling that country to defeat America.

Today, the PRC preferred to sharpen its' skill at defeating America without fighting*- just as master Sun Tzu advocated thousands of years ago. Nothing could be gained by moving forward haphazardly. Care would have to be taken to make sure others did not act precipitously.

*See *Unrestricted Warfare* by Col. Qiao Liang and Col. Wang Xiangsui (People's Liberation Army Press, 1999)

2.13

PNC CONVENTION
DENVER, COLORADO
11:10 P.M.
28 AUGUST 2008

Mallory Winston walked through the door of the receiving room of the primary suite on the penthouse floor of the Brown Palace. One of her security men stopped outside the door and the rest returned downstairs to wait after reconnoitering the route she took to the suite. Nikolay Sludtsev - the perfect host, when he chose to be - said "Congratulations my dear" in a paternal tone and handed her a glass of the red that he knew was her favorite.

Mallory had just delivered her acceptance speech for the Progressive National Committee candidacy for President of The United States. She was buoyant. This was what she had worked for her whole life. Against all odds she was here. She was elated thinking of the good she could do if she could attain this ultimate level of power. They exchanged familiar greetings and sat down on the plush leather couch.

"I always knew this moment would be yours." Nikolay flattered Winston's immense ego at the same time he deceived her. Mallory Winston believed she was Sludtsev's pick. She didn't know that Sludtsev, long ago, quit betting on any single horse. In fact she was very nearly left out in the cold.

In addition to Winston, Nikolay's groups had been backing Rick Hussain in the race to become the PNC presidential candidate. Rick had been very attractive. He was a charismatic, mixed-race candidate from Alabama. He delivered a great speech. When he attended law school in Chicago he picked up the nickname 'Bama' and it stuck with him for life. Polling showed that likely voters loved its' homey charm. Rick's childhood conversion from Islam to Christianity also played well. He came across as very palatable to older voters. They saw him as coming from a family that assimilated and embodied the American dream. Best of all, Nikolay's consultants were certain they could subtly weave Ricks non-caucasian status into a major plus with voters. They were confident a large number of non-white voters could be motivated to vote for him based on a strong empathy for his plight and a large number of white voters could be made to feel the pride of voting for America's first non-white president or the racist shame of voting against him. If managed skill-fully, Rick could be unbeatable Nikolay thought.

That was until some damned blogger reported that Rick had been a member of the Socialist Party of

America. The report was generally ignored by mainstream media, but one reporter eventually asked a follow up question on the subject. Sludtsev's groups had the dozens of blogs they controlled run definitive reports contradicting the claim. They even had a few mainstream media friends report their certainty that the claim was false; but then the other shoe dropped. Rick's campaign- already committed to an adamant denial- was confronted with the emergence of the original minutes of a January 11, 1996, Chicago chapter meeting in which Rick Hussein was sworn in as a member. Mainstream media generously treated this as a non-issue, but independent bloggers were on fire. Within days of this revelation, the man on the street no longer saw Rick's talk of redistribution of wealth and never-ending railing against "income inequality" as benign, well-intended talk. He might just be another power hungry control freak that could use a charming smile and a slippery tongue to obtain the power necessary to force you to do what he wanted, rather than have to depend upon his ability to *convince* you that he was right.

That's where Mallory came in. She had been receiving similar behind-the-scenes assistance from Sludtsev's groups. She believed she was his favorite, and when Rick unfortunately demonstrated a chink in his armor, Sludtsev smoothly tapered off his support to 'Bama'. Mallory became the favorite. Thankfully she hadn't been stupid enough to openly join a group with the word "socialist" in the title and think she could get elected by Americans.

In law school she had provided legal services to the poor. After graduation, she spent a year working on children's rights projects. Her proponents proclaimed that she could have written her own ticket, but turned down a number of lucrative job offers. She had been appointed by the President of the United States to the Legal Services Board of Directors. She served on the board of a Children's Hospital. Her husband- previous President Richard Winston- told anyone that would listen that even though she had been unsuccessful nationalizing healthcare with "Mallorycare" in 1994, she continued to struggle for the poor, helping to create the Children's Health Insurance Program (CHIP) that provided five million children health insurance, and she would never give up her quest to get medical coverage for all. She had even served as a senator.

Mallory Winston was a strong second choice, in fact she even had some of the same cards to play that Rick Hussain did. In her initial senatorial election she went up against a competitor that most people thought to be significantly more capable and experienced than she was. Her competitor made the mistake of walking up to her in a televised debate. Despite having a reputation for aggressiveness, threatening people and shouting when cameras weren't present, her supporters were able to paint the picture of a bully attempting to physically intimidate a woman. His campaign tanked. Sludtsev's people assured him that they could subtly create the media paradigm that supporting Mallory was supporting the idea of a woman president, and that opposing her was an act of reactionary sexism.

Sludtsev refilled Winston's glass. They preferred the benefit of privacy rather than to be served right now. They had a lot to discuss. They both had big plans for improving America.

Sludtsev's groups delivered more than $37 million dollars of money that he controlled to more than 527 PNC support groups. He delivered a multiple of this number with money and donors he held 'influence' over. It was worth it. Now that Blaine-Weinstein was law, nobody else was positioned to compete financially. On Tuesday November 4th, 2008, Mallory Winston was elected President of the United States.

2.14

GOETTGE FIELDHOUSE
CAMP LEJEUNE,
NORTH CAROLINA
10:15 A.M.
27 FEBRUARY 2009

President Mallory Winston stepped to her position behind the podium and looked to her teleprompter. As the agent-in-charge of her Secret Service detail stepped out of the camera frame, she began speaking to the camera in front of a crowd of Marines:

I want to acknowledge all of our soldiers, sailors, airmen and Marines serving in Iraq and Afghanistan. That includes the Camp Lejeune Marines now serving with the Second Marine Expeditionary Force in Iraq; and those with the Special Purpose Marine Air Ground Task Force in Afghanistan. We have you in our prayers. We pay tribute to your service. We thank you and your families for all that you do for America. And I want all of you to know that there is no higher honor or greater responsibility than serving as your Commander-in-Chief.

Next month will mark the sixth anniversary of the Iraq War. By any measure, this has already been a long war. For the men and women of America's armed forces – and for your families – this war has been one of the most extraordinary chapters of service in the history of our nation. You have endured tour after tour after tour of duty. You have known the dangers of combat and the loneliness of distance from loved ones. You have fought against tyranny and chaos. You have bled for your best friends and for unknown Iraqis. And you have borne an enormous burden for your fellow citizens, while extending a precious opportunity to the people of Iraq.

Today, I have come to speak to you about how the war in Iraq will end. To understand where we need to go in Iraq, it is important for the American people to understand where we now stand. Thanks in great measure to your service, the situation in Iraq has improved. Violence has been reduced substantially from the horrific sectarian killing of 2006 and 2007. Al Qaeda in Iraq has been dealt a serious blow. The capacity of Iraq's Security Forces has improved, and Iraq's leaders have taken steps toward political accommodation. The relative peace and strong participation in January's provincial elections sent a powerful message to the world about how far Iraqis have come in pursuing a peaceful political process.

The President paused. She scanned the room in front of her and looked back at her teleprompter. Clearing her throat, she continued:

Even as Iraq's government is on a surer footing, it is not yet a full partner – politically and economically – in the region, or with the international community. In short, today there is a renewed cause for hope in Iraq, but that hope rests upon an emerging foundation.

On my first full day in office, I directed my national security team to undertake a comprehensive review of our strategy in Iraq to determine the best way to strengthen that foundation, while strengthening American national security. I have listened to my Secretary of Defense, the Joint Chiefs of Staff, and commanders on the ground. We have acted with careful consideration of events on the ground; with respect for the security agreements between the United States and Iraq; and with a critical recognition that the long-term solution in Iraq must be political – not military.

We have also taken into account the simple reality that America can no longer afford to see Iraq in isolation from other priorities: we face the challenge of refocusing on Afghanistan and Pakistan; of relieving the burden on our military; and of rebuilding our struggling economy – and these are challenges that we will meet.

Today, I can announce that our review is complete, and that the United States will pursue a new strategy to end the war in Iraq through a transition to full Iraqi responsibility. This strategy is grounded in a clear and achievable goal shared by the Iraqi people and the American people: an Iraq that is sovereign, stable, and self-reliant. To achieve that goal, we will work to promote an Iraqi government that is just, representative, and accountable, and that provides neither support nor safe-haven to terrorists. We will help Iraq build new ties of trade and commerce with the world. And we will forge a partnership with the people and government of Iraq that contributes to the peace and security of the region.

President Winston took no notice as the Marines began to fidget. Every Iraq veteran below the rank of colonel wondered what Iraqi government she was talking about. They had seen few competent Iraqi soldiers and far fewer competent Iraqi units. Corruption was rampant and the cultural divide between Iraqis and these 'enlightened' ideals was huge.

What we will not do is wait for perfection. We cannot rid Iraq of all who oppose America or sympathize with our adversaries. We cannot police Iraq's streets until they are completely safe, we cannot sustain indefinitely a commitment that has put a strain on our military, and will cost the American people nearly a trillion dollars.

The first part of this strategy is therefore the responsible removal of our combat brigades from Iraq. I have chosen a timeline that will remove our combat brigades over the next 18 months. Let me say this as plainly as I can: by August 31, 2010, our combat mission in Iraq will end...

"Holy shit..." a cluster of lance corporals snickered quietly. "If we're gonna flush Iraq down the toilet, why don't we just pull out tomorrow and save a few billion?"

...So to the Iraqi people, let me be clear about America's intentions. The United States pursues no claim on your territory or your resources. We respect your sovereignty and the tremendous

sacrifices you have made for your country. We seek a full transition to Iraqi responsibility for the security of your country.

A sergeant named Green whispered to a staff sergeant to his right: "Did she just tell the bad guys that we're leaving?" The staff sergeant replied with revulsion, "She told them the day." Sgt. Green felt physically ill. Whatever adversaries stayed on the field past August 31, 2010 would automatically be the victor.

There will be more danger in the months ahead. We will face new tests and trials. But thanks to the sacrifices of those who serve, we have forged progress. We are leaving Iraq to its people, and we have begun the work of ending this war. Thank you, God Bless the United States of America, and Semper Fi.

As the President walked off, Lt Col. Killion said "I guess winning it wasn't important" sarcastically to a major named Knight. He added - "We can count on Tehran to control Baghdad on September first" - without making any attempt to avoid being overheard. "I think al Qaeda and the Sunni crews will take the Northern half of Iraq shortly after that", Knight said, stating the obvious.

2.15

UNITED STATES ATTORNEY'S OFFICE FORT STREET, DETROIT 3:05 P.M. 11 JUNE 2009

Assistant U.S. Attorney Simon Wu sat across an unremarkable wood topped desk from U.S. Attorney Rebecca Weiss. This wasn't the first time they talked over a late lunch and it wouldn't be the last Rebecca thought. She took another bite of her pastrami sandwich, wiped some mustard seeds from the corner of her mouth and asked Simon to continue.

"The Troubled Asset Relief Program (TARP) was created to preserve liquidity in the financial markets in 2008 by heading off the collapse of key financial institutions that had made fatally bad bets on real-estate securities. General Motors' (GM) financial arm was in trouble, but GM's fundamental problem was that its products were not sufficiently profitable to support its' labor expenses. The workers' union contracts with

GM prevented the carmaker from either reducing its labor costs or making its' products more efficiently. Of course, GM's management was ultimately responsible for having agreed to these unsustainable contracts," Simon said.

The previous president offered a bridge loan to GM on the condition that the company draw up a deeply revised business plan. President Winston's unique contribution, upon assuming office, was to essentially nationalize the company - without saying so - of course. The federal government violated the established bankruptcy processes and legal precedents. It protected the defective element at the center of GM's troubles: the financial interests of the union. It strong-armed GM's bondholders into accepting losses. Winston's people even construed tax law ...*creatively*...in order to discharge tens of billions of dollars in obligations that would now fall on the rest of American tax payers.

"The structured bankruptcy we would have expected by law would have required considerable governmental involvement, too," Simon continued, "but the union contracts would have been renegotiated, and GM's executive suites would have been emptied, placing the company on the road to self-sufficiency. Winston's people claim that the bailout of GM saved 1.5 million jobs. This figure is based on a supposition that if GM had gone into normal bankruptcy proceedings, all automobile manufacturing in the United States would have collapsed. Not only that, but every parts·maker, supplier, and services firm supporting the auto industry would have supposedly collapsed, too."

Of course it was unlikely that GM would have stopped production during bankruptcy; never mind the others. The assembly lines would have continued rolling, interest rates would have been cut, and union contracts would have been renegotiated in the direction of sanity. But, the U.S. government put up far more - for a 60 percent interest in GM - than it was worth. Winston regularly declared publicly that GM was "thriving," but the market didn't necessarily agree. "GM will need another bailout sooner or later," Simon opined.

Rebecca interrupted, "We have bankruptcy laws for a reason. It makes sense to expedite the proceedings for firms to prevent disruptions in the market that would harm other, healthy firms. Government control of a company is something to be feared though. That is... literally... the very definition of fascism. Who is accountable? How could efficiency or innovation ever be achieved? How could it possibly lead to anything other than cronyism and toadying to a ruler?" She stopped, realizing that she was getting into the area of expressing frustration rather than accomplishing anything.

Sufficiently comfortable with Rebecca from working many long days together, Simon pushed his glasses up and asked an indelicate question of his own. "How do you think Winston's people got these cases moved to New York?" Rebecca stood and straightened the picture of the president that government offices are required to display. She stopped and looked Mallory Winston in the eyes before replying...

2.16

PRESIDENTIAL

PALACE NO. 17

LAKE VALDAI, RUSSIA

3:40 A.M.

22 MARCH 2010

President Putin rolled and grunted in his sleep dragging silk sheets with him. "What's wrong *Zolotse?*" a sexy blonde asked lazily from behind closed eyes.

"Go back to sleep, *Kotyonok*" he said in a surprisingly caring voice. She murmured contentedly and pulled a silk sheet back over her naked breasts and up to her face.

Putin lay awake now, staring at an empty spot on the shadowed ceiling. Something was unsettling. Every morning he was given a classified intelligence summary or handed printed outline notes if he chose to forego the short verbal briefing. On this day he held onto those notes, as he had done before, and reviewed them before relaxing at the end of the day. Nothing seemed remarkable, but he knew his mind was piecing something together.

He slowly slipped out of the bed - careful not to wake the stunning 27 year old former gymnast. His eyes briefly lingered on the PVC boy shorts she was wearing before the sheet fell back into place. He sat up with his mind returning to the mystery in his head, then strode across the soft carpeted floor.

He hooked a red thong that had been abandoned by one of their guests on a toe. Pausing to remove the panties his mind demanded, "What is it?"

When he made it to the bathroom his thoughts were still churning. He stood shirtless, leaning on the marble sink. He stared into his own eyes in the mirror, preferring to keep the lights off. His thoughts kept turning to the 'Zolotov Box'.

The Zolotov Box was a piece of equipment that the KGB had used for more than a decade. It was a brilliant design that was fielded in every *rezidentura*. It was used to encrypt the most sensitive cables prior to communicating intelligence reports back to The Center in Moscow. It was one of the highest priority items to remove or destroy if a facility were going to fall into enemy hands.

Today's intelligence summary had something on the Zolotov Box in it. SVR technology officers working on an ongoing counter intelligence program had made a noteworthy discovery. It was possible to reconstruct some of the information that had passed through the box if one had access to the box. "But, so what?" They hadn't been used in decades and they were closely controlled. When they were taken out of service they were taken back to The Center by vetted couriers. Each one was then completely destroyed.

"Well not *all* of them…" *Comrade Cardinal* thought to himself. Old equipment at high-threat sites such as the Washington D.C. offices was stored since transporting it would put it in jeopardy of being compromised and exploited.

"What were the most sensitive Russian secrets that this could jeopardize if the Americans got their hands on one?… No, that wasn't the right question…" the counter intelligence people were already looking into that.

"What were the most sensitive secrets of *mine* that passed through a Zolotov Box?"

President Putin, now completely awake, asked himself where- outside of Washington D.C.- might one of these boxes have been stored rather than immediately transported and destroyed? "Well… New York…" he thought to himself.

Putin's mind was now racing. Nobody in New York had any way of knowing he had ever worked there as a case officer - he had entered and departed without reports and without anyone but Andropov's knowledge. But what about his agent? What about the man he was there to meet? They covered their tracks by having cables passed to The Center saying that he had been rejected as a source for the probability of being an American dangle. Nikolay Sludtsev's Form 21A would have gone through New York's Zolotov Box. The Americans know he had never been *their* asset. A clever analyst may well become suspicious enough to start asking questions about *Comrade Pike*.

"Ohooiet!"

Not long ago President Putin had signed an award citation for the traitorous Colonel Tretyakov. Tretyakov was the SVR's New York Station Chief. His award was for personally overseeing the destruction of New York's obsolete sensitive equipment that nobody had previously been able to get rid of. Tretyakov had personally rented a boat under a cover identity and made a number of cruises; dumping junk on each trip. The Zolotov Box Sludtsev's name went through would have been among those items and Tretyakov was now in the hands of the damned Americans.

Putin's prized asset was far too valuable to risk. If Tretyakov hadn't delivered that box to the Americans yet… and he would have no way of knowing its' value… he had damned well better be stopped! Permanently.

Comrade Cardinal turned abruptly and raced for his phone. He had an assignment for his trusted Colonel Zhukov to take care of.

2.17

THE WHITE HOUSE
WASHINGTON,
DISTRICT OF COLUMBIA
6:50 P.M.
23 MARCH 2010

President Mallory Winston leaned back in her leather chair, exhaling deeply. Three staffers had just filed out and Hillary Barrett, the President's ever professional chief of staff sat forward attentively at the edge of the couch to her side.

"..You're absolutely right..." President Winston spoke for the benefit of the speaker while Hillary quietly jotted some additional notes. President Winston - known for her thorniness by those closest to her- was in a rare mood they called "sunshine". It was for good reason. On this day she had finally signed "Mallorycare" into law. Every human being in America would have healthcare. Every one of them would have her to thank for it. Of course it had to be repackaged from her earliest attempts to nationalize healthcare so many years ago, but that was just salesmanship. There were some nitwits that didn't want the government to have any role in healthcare at all, but she understood that all reasonable people - the vast majority - wanted the government to participate for the common good.

Her message of providing oversight to control the private insurance companies and healthcare providers in the marketplace and guarantee coverage for all had previously fallen on deaf ears at the moment of truth. But, she was nothing if not tenacious. Even her sexist critics admit that.

This time around she had allies push it through the senate, and then the house promising the law would lower everyone's costs and bolster the national economy that was still stumbling after those fools on Wall Street had been permitted to run wild in 2008. If not for the quick-wittedness of her people and her decisive action, the United States would have fallen into a depression more severe than that of the 1920s and taken the world with it. She still marveled at the damage America could do to others... but she had been elected with a mandate to correct that.

If she had erred, it was in not reaching far enough. If she had been able to get larger blocks of stimulus funds approved, she could have exerted greater control, and the economy would be booming right now. Regardless - "Mallorycare" was law. The Patient Protection and Affordable Care Act, as it was officially titled, would be the keystone to the initiatives that enabled Mallory Winston to bring the country out of the dark ages.

With more influence to wield over the people and greater control of the nation's assets and resources, she could do more good. By doing more good, she would acquire more influence over people and more control over assets. It was a circular process that served the common good of all people...and not just Americans for once. It infuriated her that there were those who would deliberately spin that paradigm as something fearful.

"...The second meeting is next month..." Mallory elaborated with part of her mind still pre-occupied with the day's achievement.

On the surface, all Mallorycare did was to: preclude insurance companies from denying coverage for pre-existing medical conditions; provide minimum standards of coverage that the insurance sharks would have to meet; require everyone to buy an insurance policy and provide subsidies for the poor to obtain their policies. This was hardly the Orwellian plot that her reactionary critics claimed.

Even though lowering costs wasn't exactly the main point; even positive financial benefits could be achieved if one looked at it from the right perspective. If private sector employers dumped their employee's health benefits under these circumstances that would prove them to be the self-serving Capitalists that they were. Furthermore, if that just *happened* to occur, it would provide a national uproar *demanding* national healthcare. The President's staff had assured her that there may be many balls left on the table, but after the next shot, they would fall in sequence and the eight ball would be in the corner pocket.

"Nikolay, I couldn't have done this without your help," the President said into the speaker sincerely.

The Act and its' regulations were 11,000 pages long. A key senator Mallory counted on to push it forward even made the accidentally true public remark, "We have to pass the bill, so you can find out what's in it."

Experts from several of the relevant think tanks of the Free Community Partnership had crafted some of the supporting provisions. The administrative work alone would have clogged up Mallory's staff or anyone else's. She appreciated the grunt work Nikolay's people had done with the unglamorous job of turning ideas into words.

"President Winston," Nikolay flattered, using the title he rarely spoke, "For as long as you struggle for common people... to right the wrongs of the past... and to champion diversity and tolerance," he parroted her favorite buzzwords, "I will be honored to stand at your side." He delivered the sentence as sincerely as he could muster and the phone call was ended.

Mallory took a deep breath. Nick Sludtsev was a kindred spirit. They both had high aspirations for the service they could render humankind within their lifetimes, and Nick put his money where his mouth was. What an amazing man.

"Hillary... you ran one of Nick's Free Community Partnership groups for a time before starting work with my campaign...didn't you?" Mallory Winston asked wistfully.

2.18

PANDORA ESTATES

TAMPA, FLORIDA

4:25 P.M. 13 JUNE 2010

A large brown shipping truck turned right approaching the Pandora Estates guardhouse. The driver, a 30-something blonde sat behind the wheel in the unique, almost standing position the truck required. She wore a frumpy brown uniform with shorts and a button down shirt; but that didn't prevent the 48 year old part-time security guard from noticing the beauty's striking resemblance to actress Samantha Saint.

The chubby guard regretted the fact that he was instructed to automatically wave delivery trucks through. He would have enjoyed chatting with this angel even if just for a moment. Orders were orders though and he pressed the button that raised the gate giving a friendly wave at the same time. The driver gave a warm partial smile and accelerated toward the gate arm as it raised.

She splashed through the scattered puddles that served as evidence of the most recent afternoon thunderstorm. The truck made a left turn and the driver counted down the house numbers. She brought the vehicle to a stop in front of a large two-story house and inched forward until her truck was centered on the tall front windows. After retrieving a large, reinforced envelope from the back of the truck the delivery person strode confidently toward the front door.

She passed through a split flower garden looking left and right and knocked loudly on the door. She could feel the gaze of a person checking her out through the peep hole for a few moments before the door opened. She smiled disarmingly at the middle-aged man that opened the door.

He was taken aback by both her beauty and the Florida humidity that hit him when he leaned out. She had a large envelope under her arm and held out a pen and clipboard to the resident. Part of his mind began to question why she had an old fashioned paper receipt when the modern world had transitioned to electronic signatures.

"Sir, can you sign please?" she said invitingly.

He didn't notice that she had quickly paced his breathing. As he reached for the pen she pulled it back oddly with the spring loaded button toward her shoulder. He stared into the opening of the pen momentarily perplexed when she pressed the actuator and compressed gas blew a cloud of Succinylcholine mist into his face. It was perfectly timed with his inhalation.

She stepped back as he coughed once and sank to his knees. She tore the end off the envelope as if rehearsed and unhesitatingly pulled a single photocopied page from within. The man's hands moved to his throat and he fell to a fetal position. She placed the paper in his hand and closed his dormant fingers around it. The man lost control of his muscles and he watched, conscious, but paralyzed as the terror of what was happening penetrated his mind.

The delivery person produced an iPhone and pressed two quick photos of her victim. She spun on her heel and strode away decisively. Concealed from view by the placement of her truck she made her way to the driver's seat. The delivery woman efficiently started the engine and pulled away. She made her way deliberately through the housing development driving exactly the posted speed limits. In moments she was past the guardhouse- never having had to make eye contact with the guard on duty again.

Late morning on the following day, Hillsborough County Sheriff's Deputies found the delivery truck abandoned in a parking lot of the International Plaza and Bay Street Mall. The coroner's report indicated that the 53 year old Caucasian male died from sudden cardiac arrest.

The page grasped in his lifeless hand was a photocopy of a news article written in Russian. The article was pre-dated 26 July 2010 and quoted Russian President Vladimir Putin as having said that doom was "the ultimate fate to befall traitors" on 24 July, 2010. Colonel Sergei Tretyakov, former SVR New York Chief of Station, defector, and freshly minted United States citizen died at home on 13 June, 2010.

2.19

THE WHITE HOUSE
WASHINGTON,
DISTRICT OF COLUMBIA
3:20 P.M.
25 JANUARY 2011

President Mallory Winston adjusted a bracelet below the podium and looked up. She looked straight into the camera and paused momentarily before speaking. She said:

Good evening. Over the past few days the American people have watched the situation unfolding in Egypt. We've seen enormous demonstrations. We are witness to the beginning of a new chapter in the history of a great country, and a long-time friend of the United States. My administration has been in close contact with our Egyptian counterparts and a broad range of the Egyptian people, and others across the region and across the globe. I must make clear the following:

First, we oppose violence, and I want to commend the Egyptian military for the professionalism and patriotism that it has shown thus far in allowing peaceful protests while protecting the Egyptian people. We've seen tanks covered with banners and soldiers and protesters embracing in the streets. In the future, I urge the military to continue its efforts to help ensure that this time of change is peaceful.

Second, we stand for universal values, including the rights of the Egyptian people to freedom of assembly, freedom of speech, the freedom to access information and the freedom from want for all people. Once more, we've seen the incredible potential for technology to empower citizens and the dignity of those who stand up for a better future. The United States will continue to stand up for democratic principles and the universal rights that all human beings deserve in Egypt and around the world.

Third, I am speaking out on the need for change. After his speech tonight, I spoke directly to Egyptian President Hosni Mubarak. I told him that the status quo is not sustainable and that a change must take place. Through thousands of years Egypt has known many moments of transformation and this is one such moment. I told President Mubarak that he must step down.

"Oh, my God" Special Agent Cynthia Grey of the Diplomatic Security Service thought to herself. She caught President Winston's words on a television in her Miami office, and immediately gasped. Not two weeks earlier, she had served on the detail protecting President Mubarak as he was honored by Mallory Winston at a state dinner in Washington.

Now, it is not the role of any other country to determine Egypt's leaders, only the Egyptian people can do that. What is clear and what I indicated tonight to President Mubarak is my belief that an orderly transition must be meaningful, it must be peaceful, and it must begin now. Furthermore it also must include a broad spectrum of voices and opposition parties.

Captain Massri looked over, pale faced, at Sergeant Chalthoum. The two Egyptian soldiers saw the American President's speech on a television through the bars of a shop window. They couldn't hear her, but they could read the caption. "Does she not know that the 'opposition' will be controlled by the islamists? Does she not know that there is nobody but the army sufficiently organized to stand up to them? Has she not seen flags from all the different terrorist groups being flown within the crowds?" the sergeant asked quietly. They may not have been the majority, but when three wolves and ten sheep are voting on what to have for dinner, the menu is quite predictable.

It should lead to elections that are fair, and it should result in a government that's not only grounded in democracy, but is also responsive to the aspirations of the diverse Egyptian people. Throughout this process, the United States will continue to extend the hand of partnership and friendship to Egypt, and we stand ready to provide any assistance that's necessary to help the Egyptian people as they manage the aftermath of these protests. Over the last few days, the passion and the dignity that has been demonstrated by the people of Egypt has been an inspiration to people around the world, including here in the United States, and to all those who believe in the inevitability of human freedom.

"President Winston just fired the President of Egypt," CIA watch officer Kevin Johnson said to the three interns in his Langley office. The interns may not have grasped the significance, but Kevin certainly understood that now made the United States responsible for all the events to come in Egypt...and beyond... in the minds of millions of people. "Expect high traffic tomorrow. There's going to be quite a bit of contingency planning going on," he said evenly.

To the people of Egypt, especially the young people, I want to be clear. I hear your voices. I have an unyielding belief that you will determine your own destiny and seize the promise of a better future for your children and your grandchildren. I say that as someone who is committed to a partnership with you. There will be difficult days ahead. Many questions about Egypt's future remain unanswered, but I am confident that the people of Egypt will find those answers. That truth can be seen in the sense of community in the streets. It can be seen in the families embracing soldiers, and it can be seen in the Egyptians who linked arms. A new generation moving ever 'forward'. A human chain connecting a great and ancient civilization to the promise of a new day. Thank you very much. God Bless the United States of America.

2.20

CROCKETT STREET
WACO, TEXAS
7:15 A.M.
5 FEBRUARY 2011

Juana Lopez walked distractedly from the weathered mail box toward the front door of her small home. She enjoyed the feel of dewy grass on her bare feet and the light breeze in her long black hair. She shuffled through the envelopes and came to one addressed to 'Grupo Educación Constitucional'. This was the non-profit group that she and her husband were working to launch. After waiting four years to come to the United States, they were both, finally, proud new citizens. They had been fascinated by the U.S. Constitution and the Bill of Rights. No other country had anything like this to limit the powers of the elite over citizens. They wanted to share what they were learning with other new citizens. The letter looked important. She tore into it anxiously...

Internal Revenue Service
P.O. Box 2508
Cincinnati, OH 45201
Date: January 26, 2011

Response Due Date:
February 05, 2011

Dear Sir or Madam:

We need more information before we can complete our consideration of your application for exemption. Please provide the information requested on the enclosed Information Request by the response due date shown above, Your response must be signed by an authorized person or an officer whose name is listed on your application, Also, the information you submit should be accompanied by the following declaration:

Under penalties of perjury, 1 declare that 1 have examined this information, including accompanying documents, and, to the best of my knowledge and belief the information contains all the relevant facts relating to the request/or the information, and such facts are true, correct, and complete.

Juana thought this sounded a little threatening. She read on...

If we approve your application for exemption, we will be required by law to make the application and the information that you submit in response to this letter available for public inspection.

She skipped down to the list of questions...

1. Do you directly or indirectly communicate with members of legislative bodies? If so, provide copies of the written communications and contents of other forms of communications. Please include the percentage of time and resources you have spent or will spend conducting these activities in relation to 100% of all your activities, and the names of the donors, contributors, and grantors.

a) How did you use these donations, contributions, and grants? Provide the details. If you did not receive or do not expect to receive any, please confirm by answering this question "None received" and/or "None expected"

b) The amounts of membership income received for each year. If you did not receive or do not expect to receive any membership income, please confirm by answering this question "None received" and/or "None expected"

c) The amounts of fundraising income received for each year. If you did not receive or do not expect to receive any fundraising income, please confirm by answering this question "None received" and/or "None expected".

d) The amounts of any other incomes received for each year. If you did not receive or do not expect to receive any other incomes, please confirm by answering this question "None received" and/or "None expected".

Juana knew her husband had provided all of this in the past- several times – each time it was requested.

2. Provide the following information for the expenses you have incurred for the years from inception to the present. Also: provide the same information for the expenses you expect to incur for 2012, 2013, and 2014.

a) Donation, contribution, and grant expenses for each year which includes the following information:

• *The names of the donees, recipients, and grantees. If the donee, recipient, or grantee has run or will run for a public office, identify the office. If not, please confirm by answering this question "No".*

• *The amounts of each of the donations, contributions, and grants and the dates you donated, contributed, or granted them.*

• *The amounts of each of the donations, contributions, and grants and the dates you expect to donate, contribute, or grant them.*

• *Provide the reasons for issuing the donations, contributions. and grants.*

If you did not issue or do not expect to issue receive any donations, contributions. and grants, please confirm by answering this question "None to be provided".

b) Compensation, salary, wage and reimbursement expenses for each year.

How could she possibly know if anyone that had helped them would ever run for office?

3. Do you encourage eligible voters to educate themselves, register to vote, and vote?

a) Explain in detail how you do this, For example, do you conduct voter registration or get out the vote drives, or voter education?

b) In the course of conducting these activities do your members or volunteers urge the voters to support or oppose particular candidates or slates of candidates?

c) If not, describe how you ensure that these activities are conducted in a strictly nonpartisan manner.

Of course they did. They had already reported time and time again that they encouraged citizens to vote to support enforcement of the U.S Constitution. They thought they were following in the footsteps of Frederick Douglass the former slave that had become an ardent supporter of the Bill of Rights. They weren't revolutionaries or insurgents. Their organization was intended to safeguard against politicians who try to circumvent the Bill of Rights and to protect the voting process from unscrupulous attempts to "get-out-the-illegal-alien-vote" that she had witnessed. The IRS knew this. She had read the letters her husband had sent them.

4. Provide copies of any agreements you have with others for provision of goods or services, sharing of facilities or other cooperative arrangements, or anything else.

5. What percentage of your time is devoted to each of the following? What percentage of your resources?

a) Member events In which electoral issues, including the qualifications of candid8tes or slates of candidates are also discussed.

b) Organization/participation in public events. Within this category, what percentage involved some kind of intervention in the political process, including, but not exclusively, express or implicit endorsement or opposition to candidates or slates of candidates.

c) Express endorsements of candidates through press releases, advertising, member communications, radio shows, or other media.

d) Financial. or other support to candidates, slates of candidates, or political parties.

e) Voter education and engagement activities which tend to support or oppose specific candidates or slates of candidates.

f) Issue-related advocacy communications, Within this category, what percentage Include comparisons of the positions of candidates or slates of candidates on these issues with your positions?

g) Compilation and distribution of candidate questionnaires, voter guides. Incumbent or candidate ratings, and so forth.

h) Member events in which only legislative issues are discussed.

i) Nonpartisan voter education or engagement activities.

j) Fundraising.

k) Website maintenance.

6. Other administrative, including officer travel and participation in conferences. Please describe fully. Submit the following information relating to your past and present directors, officers, and key employees:

a) Provide a resume for each.

b) Indicate the number of hours per month each individual has provided or is providing services to you.

e) Provide a description of all the services each individual provides or has provided to you.

d) Indicate the total compensation provided to each individual.

f) Describe how each compensation package was determined.

g) Indicate if any of your current and former officers, directors, and key employees are related to each other (include family and business relation ships) and describe the nature of the relationship.

7. *List each past or present board member, officer, key employee and members of their families who:*

a) Has served on the board of your organization.

b) Was, is or plans to be a candidate for public office. Indicate the nature of each candidacy.

c) Has previously conducted similar activities for another entity.

d) Has previously submitted an application for tax exempt status.

8. *Provide copies of all communications, pamphlets, advertisements, and other materials distributed by the organization regarding the legislation*

a) A vendor list. Indicate if the vendor is a related party.

b) A list of items sold.

c) Your cost for each item.

d) The selling price of each item.

9. *Regarding your current and planned employees:*

a) How many employees do you have?

b) Indicate the total of full - time, part-time, and seasonal employees.

c) If employees are part- time, when did/do they work?

d) If employees are seasonal, during what season (month) did/do they work?

e) How many employees are/were devoted to each activity of the organization throughout the year?

10. Will you conduct educational events, discussion groups or similar events. For each event you have conducted:

a) Indicate the date and location.

b) Describe the nature of the event.

c) Provide copies of all materials distributed with regards to the event.

d) List all event revenue.

e) List all event expenses

11. Have any candidates for public office spoken at a function of the organization other than a candidate forum? If yes, provide the following:

a) The names of the candidates.

b) The functions at which they spoke.

c) Any materials distributed or published with regard to their appearance and the event.

d) Any video or audio recordings of ths event.

e) A transcript of any speeches given by the candidate(s).

12. Have you conducted or will you conduct voter education activities (voter registration drives, get out the vote drives, publishing voter guides, distributing voter guides etc ...)? If yes:

a) provide the location, date and time of the events.

b) Who on the organization's behalf has or will conduct the voter registration or get out the vote drives?

c) How many resources (funds/volunteers) are devoted to the activity?

d) Provide copies of all materials published or distributed regarding the activities, including copies of any voter guides.

13. Has your organization engaged in any activities with the news media? If so, please describe those activities in further detail and, provide copies of articles printed or transcripts of items aired. That activity may include the following:

a) Press releases.

b) Interviews with news media.

c) Letters to the editor.

d) Op-ed pieces.

Juana was perplexed. She knew her husband sent everything requested several times over before getting this letter. Now they were being asked for details no reasonable person could ever have recorded. She wondered if the groups advocating *against* the U.S. Constitution and encouraging politicians to ignore the Bill of Rights received the same letter. They might have, she thought, but she wondered if they were strung along with requests to provide such tiny details for questions they had already answered. She and her husband had never been turned down, but...

If you have any questions, please contact the person whose name and telephone number are shown in the heading of this letter.

This made no sense. The letter was unsigned. There was no phone number.

Sincerely yours,

Exempt Organizations Specialist
Enclosure: Information Request

2.21

THE WHITE HOUSE
WASHINGTON,
DISTRICT OF COLUMBIA
7:35 P.M.
7 FEBRUARY 2011

President Mallory Winston stepped toward the camera and began speaking immediately. Looking directly at the audience, she spoke evenly and with authority. "Tonight, I must update the American people on the effort that I have undertaken in Libya – what we've done, and why this matters to us." She scanned her teleprompter and continued:

As we speak, our troops are helping our ally Japan recover from their tsunami, leaving Iraq to its people, and stopping the Taliban's momentum in Afghanistan. As Commander-in-Chief, I'm grateful to our soldiers, sailors, airmen, Marines, coast guardsmen, and to their families. For generations, the

United States of America has played a unique role as an anchor of global security and as an advocate for human freedom. When our interests and values are at stake, we have a responsibility to act. That's what happened in Libya.

Libya sits directly between Tunisia and Egypt - two nations that inspired the world when their people rose up to take control of their own destiny. For more than four decades, the Libyan people have been ruled by a tyrant – Muammar Qaddafi. He has denied his people freedom, exploited their wealth, murdered opponents at home and abroad, and terrorized innocent people around the world – including Americans who were killed by Libyan agents.

"…And assisted the U.S. government in chasing down al Qaeda and Islamic supremacist militants from the other groups…" Colonel Ken Smith of the Defense Intelligence Agency said to his television. Qaddafi was a snake and he had killed Americans. He deserved a bullet to be sure, but in a world boiling over with Islamist instigation, this seemed like an odd time to turn away anyone willing to assist.

Last month, Qaddafi's grip of fear appeared to give way to the promise of freedom. In cities and towns across the country, Libyans took to the streets to claim their basic human rights. Faced with this opposition, Qaddafi began attacking his people. As President, I took a series of swift steps in a matter of days to answer Qaddafi's aggression. We froze more than $30 billion of Qaddafi's assets. Joining with the United Nations Security Council, we broadened our sanctions, imposed an arms embargo, and enabled Qaddafi to be held accountable *for their crimes. I made it clear that Qaddafi had lost the confidence of his people and the legitimacy to lead, and I said that he needed to step down from power.*

Qaddafi chose to escalate his attacks, launching a military campaign against the Libyan people. Innocent people were targeted for killing. Hospitals and ambulances were attacked. Journalists were arrested, sexually assaulted, and killed. Supplies of food and fuel were choked off. Water for hundreds of thousands of people was shut off. Cities and towns were shelled, mosques were destroyed, and apartment buildings reduced to rubble.

I ordered warships into the Mediterranean. European allies declared their willingness to commit resources to stop the killing. The Libyan opposition and the Arab League appealed to the world to save lives in Libya. And so at my direction, America led an effort with our allies at the United Nations to pass a resolution that authorized a no-fly zone to stop the regime's air attacks, and further authorized all necessary measures to protect the Libyan people.

The United States had no choice. We saw regime forces on the outskirts of the city. We knew that if we waited...just one more day, Benghazi could suffer a massacre that would reverberate across the region and stain the conscience of the world. It was not in our national interest to let that happen. Nine days ago, after consulting with the United Nations, I authorized military action.

The Director of Central Intelligence rolled his eyes from his television to the ceiling. "You fired more than 100 cruise missiles at Libyans is what you did." The director was not thrilled to have a war of such questionable value started. "Now you own Libya's can of worms" he thought to himself alluding to the Islamist free-for-all sure to follow the loss of Qadaffi.

We struck forces approaching Benghazi to save that city and the people within it. We hit Qaddafi's troops in neighboring Ajdabiya, allowing the opposition to drive them out. We targeted tanks and military assets that had been choking off towns and cities, and we cut off much of their source of supply...tonight, I can report that we have stopped Qaddafi's deadly advance. In this effort, I have not acted alone. I have been joined by nations like France, Canada, Denmark, Norway, Italy, Spain, Greece, and Turkey- and Arab partners like Qatar and the United Arab Emirates.

I said that America's role would be limited; that we would transfer responsibility to our allies and partners. Tonight, we are fulfilling that pledge. So for those who doubted our capacity to carry out this operation, I want to be clear: The United States of America has done what we said we would do.

Tomorrow, my secretary of state will go to London, where she will meet with the Libyan freedom fighters and consult with more than 30 nations. These discussions will focus on the goal of a Libya that belongs not to a dictator, but to its people. In fact, much of the debate in Washington has put forward a false choice when it comes to Libya. On the one hand, some question why America should intervene at all – even in non-decisive ways. They argue that there are many places in the world where innocent civilians face brutal violence at the hands of their government, and America cannot police the world.

That cannot be an argument for not acting. To brush aside America's responsibility to the global community would be wrong. America had an important strategic interest in preventing Qaddafi from overrunning those freedom fighters. A massacre would have driven thousands of additional refugees across Libya's borders, putting enormous strains on the peaceful transitions in Egypt and Tunisia. The democratic impulses that are dawning across the region would be eclipsed by the darkest form of dictatorship. The writ of the United Nations Security Council would have been shown to be little more than empty words, crippling that institution's future credibility to uphold global peace and security. Let me close by addressing what this action says about America's leadership in the world, under my presidency.

U.S. Air Force Academy Cadet Jennifer Dominguez looked down from the rec. room television in her dorm in Colorado Springs. She wondered what the *real* point was. If the United States went to war every time a dictator, warlord or thug threatened his own people, the country would be perpetually at war. No economy could sustain that. "When Qadaffi is gone, won't the Islamist gangs bent on world domination be left in control?" she asked herself.

As Commander-in-Chief, I have no greater responsibility than keeping this country safe. And no decision weighs on me more than when to deploy our men and women in uniform. I've made it clear that I will never hesitate to use our military swiftly, decisively, and unilaterally when necessary to defend our people and our interests. That is why we continue to fight in Afghanistan, even as we have ended our combat mission in Iraq and removed more than 100,000 troops from that country. There will be times, though, when our safety is not directly threatened, but our interests are.

My fellow Americans, I know that at a time of upheaval overseas - when the news is filled with conflict- it can be tempting to turn away from the world. But as I've said before, our strength abroad is anchored in our strength at home. That must always be our North Star - the ability of our people to progress to their potential, to collectively make wise choices with our resources, and to share the prosperity that serves as a wellspring for our power.

Thank you. God bless the United States of America.

Mallory Winston looked down from the camera and concluded her speech. She turned to leave and took a step forward. She was proud of her delivery.

2.22

THE CAPITOL
WASHINGTON,
DISTRICT OF COLUMBIA
11:35 A.M.
10 FEBRUARY 2011

Senator Jim Blaine sat quietly, flipping through a yellow legal pad full of hand written notes. He had been invited to attend the day's proceedings personally by a member of the Congressional Anti-Terrorism Caucus. All eyes were on the bald Director of National Intelligence, James Clapper. He sat uneasily scanning the cameras and crowd through his glasses. Clapper cleared his throat and continued speaking.

"Let me just speak briefly..." the DNI said buying himself another second of time with a cough "to the Mu...uh...Muslim Brotherhood..." he said behind a rapid fire sequence of facial ticks "as an international... uh...movement." He continued, "And then I'll ask

Director Mueller to speak specifically to it here...uh... domestically. Umm...the reason I do that of course is... uh... because the Muslim Brotherhood is prominent now in what's going on now in Egypt and elsewhere in the mid-East. The...the term 'Muslim Brotherhood'...is an umbrella term..." he said gesturing feebly, "...for a variety of movements, in the case of Egypt...uh...a very heterogeneous group, largely secular...secular..."

Senator Blaine's jaw nearly hit the floor. He scribbled quickly on his pad and nudged the Caucus member's assistant beside him. She looked down and read, "WTF?! Bin Laden was Brotherhood/Zawahiri was Brotherhood" Blaine wrote referring to the fact that the key al Qaeda leaders and key figures of virtually all Sunni Muslim terrorist groups had either been radicalized by - or studied ideology from - The Brotherhood.

The Senator continued scribbling as Clapper continued speaking. The DNI claimed "...which has eschewed violence and has decried al Qaeda as a perversion of Islam."

"Is this guy stoned? On MB's payroll?" Blaine's notepad flashed. The fact that the Muslim Brotherhood had been active in assassinations, political subversion and other nefarious deeds over the decades was a matter of fact on the public record. It was open source knowledge available to anyone. It didn't require a top secret clearance to have known that. There were squabbles within The Brotherhood to be sure, but The Brotherhood was unified in its' vision of Islamic supremacism, conquest and subjugation of all others. Some Brotherhood alumni became subversive activists, some alumni became mujahedeen - 'soldiers of God'. Blaine wondered what kind of idiot would consider this objective legitimate merely because it originated from the political side of the house rather than the "military" side.

"They have pursued…uh…social…uhh…ends, a betterment of the political order in Egypt…umm…and et cetera.....In other countries, there are also chapters or franchises of the Muslim Brotherhood, but there is no overarching agenda, particularly in pursuit of violence, at least internationally…" Clapper stuttered on.

The congressional assistant, a former FBI special-agent-in-charge, leaned in and whispered to Blaine, "The Muslim Brotherhood's motto is: *Allah is our objective. The Prophet is our leader. The Koran is our law. Jihad is our way. Dying in the way of Allah is our highest hope.*" She went on…"The Muslim Brotherhood's founder, Hassan al-Banna wrote: *It is in the nature of Islam to dominate, not to be dominated, to impose its law on all nations and to extend its power to the entire planet.*"

After Clapper's testimony was complete, Jim Blaine and former FBI SAC Julie McCarthy returned to the senator's office. He poured an icy Coca-Cola into the whiskey glass in front of her and then topped off his own glass. "What do you think is going on here?" he asked.

"I've never seen anything like this" she said.

"Is somebody running him as an asset?" Senator Blaine asked sincerely using the terminology of an intelligence officer.

"I've never seen anything like this" the congressional assistant repeated evenly. "His statements were false and misleading. They were provided in sworn testimony to the Congress."

"Is it possible that he thought what he was saying was true?" Blaine interrupted with the question.

"I don't see how that could be. Anyone with a working knowledge of world history would know better than that. He's not just *anybody*; he's the Director of National Intelligence." Blaine's guest said soberly.

"He's an agent-of-influence then?" the senator asked quietly. Julie could not answer that question. Blaine thanked her and made certain that she had a direct number for him. "What was the president thinking allowing this guy to serve as Director of National Intelligence?" he asked himself silently.

After staring out the window motionless for several moments, he spun in his chair. He began drafting a letter to the Attorney General of the United States. This was one hell of a mess. McCarthy was certain that Clapper's misleading statements would catch fire on YouTube. This would no doubt lead the evening news. Blaine was confident that the President would ask for the DNI's resignation. He would be gone within 72 hours. This letter was the senator's way of doing his part. He was providing Mallory Winston one more piece of leverage to justify doing the right thing…doing what had to be done…there really wasn't any other choice for her…was there?

2.23

THE WHITE HOUSE
WASHINGTON,
DISTRICT OF COLUMBIA
11:35 P.M. 2 MAY 2011

President Mallory Winston stepped to the microphone and said, "Good evening…Tonight, I can report to the American people and to the world that the United States has conducted an operation that killed Osama bin Laden, the leader of al Qaeda, and a terrorist who's responsible for the murder of thousands of innocent men, women, and children." She continued:

It was nearly 10 years ago that a bright September day was darkened by the worst attack on the American people in our history. The images of 9/11 are seared into our national memory… hijacked planes cutting through a cloudless September sky; the Twin Towers collapsing to the ground; black smoke billowing up from the Pentagon; the wreckage of Flight 93 in

Shanksville, Pennsylvania, where the actions of heroic citizens saved us from even more heartbreak and destruction.

And yet we know that the worst images are those that were unseen to the world... the empty seat at the dinner table; children who were forced to grow up without their mother or their father; parents who would never know the feeling of their child's embrace; nearly 3,000 citizens taken from us, leaving a gaping hole in our hearts.

On September 11, 2001, in our time of grief, the American people came together. We offered our neighbors a hand, and we offered the wounded our blood. We reaffirmed our ties to each other, and our love of community and country. On that day, no matter where we came from, what God we prayed to, or what race or ethnicity we were, we were united as one American family.

We were also united in our resolve to protect our nation and to bring those who committed this vicious attack to justice. We quickly learned that the 9/11 attacks were carried out by al Qaeda – an organization headed by Osama bin Laden, which had openly declared war on the United States and was committed to killing innocents in our country and around the globe. And so we went to war against al Qaeda to protect our citizens, our friends, and our allies.

Over the last ten years, thanks to the tireless and heroic work of our military and our counterterrorism profession-als, we've made great strides in that effort. We've disrupted terrorist attacks and strengthened our homeland defense. In Afghanistan, we removed the Taliban government, which had given bin Laden and al Qaeda safe haven and support. And around the globe, we worked with our friends and allies to capture or kill scores of al Qaeda terrorists, including several who were a part of the 9/11 plot.

President Winston quickly scanned ahead and continued, "Yet Osama bin Laden avoided capture and escaped across the Afghan border into Pakistan. Meanwhile, al Qaeda continued to operate from along that border and operate through its affiliates across the world. And so shortly after taking office, I…directed the director of the CIA, to make the killing or capture of bin Laden the top priority of our war against al Qaeda, even as we continued our broader efforts to disrupt, dismantle, and defeat his network." This wasn't exactly true…but she had never *rescinded* the previous president's order.

She continued, "Then, last August, after years of painstaking work by our intelligence community, I was briefed on a possible lead to bin Laden. It was far from certain, and it took many months to run this thread to ground. I met repeatedly with my national security team as we developed more information about the possibility that we had located bin Laden hiding within a compound deep inside Pakistan. And finally, last week, I determined that we had enough intelligence to take action, and authorized an operation to get Osama bin Laden and bring him to justice." President Winston masked her emotions. She had actually withheld a decision. Two of her most trusted advisors were convinced that this attack would provoke the Muslim world. They insisted it would end up embarrassing her.

"Today, at my…direction, the United States launched a targeted operation against that compound in Abbottabad, Pakistan. A small team of Americans carried out the operation with extraordinary courage and capability. No

Americans were harmed. They took care to avoid civilian casualties. After a firefight, they killed Osama bin Laden and took custody of his body." The President had to relax her grip when she realized the tension she was expressing thinking about the fact that her CIA director okayed the raid and only told her after it was underway. He had claimed that they thought bin Laden was leaving and had to act immediately. She knew this was a lie.

For over two decades, bin Laden has been al Qaeda's leader and symbol, and has continued to plot attacks against our country and our friends and allies. The death of bin Laden marks the most significant achievement to date in our nation's effort to defeat al Qaeda. Yet his death does not mark the end of our effort. There's no doubt that al Qaeda will continue to pursue attacks against us. We must...and we will...remain vigilant at home and abroad.

As we do, we must also reaffirm that the United States is not...and never will be...at war with Islam. I've made clear, that our war is not against Islam. Bin Laden was not a Muslim leader; he was a mass murderer of Muslims. Indeed, al Qaeda has slaughtered scores of Muslims in many countries, including our own. So his demise should be welcomed by all who believe in peace and human dignity.

Over the years, I've repeatedly made clear that we would take action within Pakistan if we knew where bin Laden was. That is what we've done. But it's important to note that our counterterrorism cooperation with Pakistan helped lead us to bin Laden and the compound where he was hiding. Indeed, bin Laden had declared war against Pakistan as well, and ordered attacks against the Pakistani people.

Tonight...I called President Zardari, and my team has also spoken with their Pakistani counterparts. They agree that this is a good and historic day for both of our nations. And going forward, it is essential that Pakistan continue to join us in the fight against al Qaeda and its affiliates.

The American people did not choose this fight. It came to our shores, and started with the senseless slaughter of our citizens. After nearly ten years of service, struggle, and sacrifice, we know well the costs of war. These efforts weigh on me every time I, as Commander-in-Chief, have to sign a letter to a family that has lost a loved one, or look into the eyes of a service member who's been gravely wounded.

So Americans understand the costs of war. Yet as a country, we will never tolerate our security being threatened, nor stand idly by when our people have been killed. We will be relentless in defense of our citizens and our friends and allies. We will be true to the values that make us who we are. And on nights like this one, we can say to those families who have lost loved ones to al Qaeda's terror: justice has been done.

Tonight, we give thanks to the countless intelligence and counterterrorism professionals who've worked tirelessly to achieve this outcome. The American people do not see their work, nor know their names. But tonight, they feel the satisfaction of their work and the result of their pursuit of justice.

We give thanks for the men who carried out this operation, for they exemplify the professionalism, patriotism, and unparalleled courage of those who serve our country. And they are part of a generation that has borne the heaviest share of the burden since that September day.

Finally, let me say to the families who lost loved ones on 9/11 that we have never forgotten your loss, nor wavered in our commitment to see that we do whatever it takes to prevent another attack on our shores. And tonight, let us think back to the sense of unity that prevailed on 9/11. I know that it has, at times, frayed. Yet today's achievement is a testament to the greatness of our country and the determination of the American people.

"The cause of securing our country is not complete. But tonight, we are…once again reminded that America can do whatever we set our mind to. That is the story of our history, whether it's the pursuit of prosperity for our people, or the struggle for equality for all our citizens; our commitment to stand up for our values abroad, and our sacrifices to make the world a safer place. Let us remember that we can do these things not just because of wealth or power, but because of who we are: one nation, under God, indivisible, with liberty and justice for all. Thank you. May God bless you, and may God bless the United States of America." The crap she had to shovel to superstitious American yokels was ridiculous. She couldn't wait until she could quit spewing this nonsense after the next election. However, as much as she hated it, she couldn't afford to miss claiming credit for a successful mission that would be *this* popular.

2.24

GIZA STREET STUDIO
CAIRO, EGYPT
10:10 A.M. 3 JUNE 2011

Mohamed Morsi, chairman of Egypt's brand new 'Freedom and Justice Party' leaned in to hear what his colleague was saying. On the other side of the table, a shaved headed man with dark framed glasses and a C. Everett Koop beard continued speaking.

"…35% of Ethiopians belong to the Oromo people. They have a thing called the Oromo Liberation Front. The domestic Ethiopian front is weak and fragile… We can also support the Ogaden National Liberation Front. This would constitute a means to pressure the Ethiopian government…"

An assistant to Mr. Morsi touched him on the shoulder. When he turned slightly, the man whispered, "The American Secretary of State has requested a meeting with you…"

Another party chairman with a striking resemblance to actor Paul Sorvino pushed up his wire rim glasses and interjected, "I don't know whether this is something that should be said or not, but like some of my colleagues said, there are many political rivalries in Ethiopian society...We need a task force that will deal with politics and intelligence. We should play a role in all aspects of Ethiopian reality. I think this would be much less costly than other options...we should intervene in their domestic affairs. We can leak intelligence information. We can make them believe we are buying war planes..."

Mohamed Morsi *knew* this moment would come, and he found it quite sweet indeed. Five months ago he was a prisoner in the terrorist wing of the Wadi al Natrun prison. Brothers from HAMAS and Hezbollah liberated the prison at the same time that riots overwhelmed the Mubarak government and the world press celebrated the 'Arab Spring'.

A fourth party chairman in a grey suit and striped tie also spoke up, "...we should form an axis with Eritrea, Somalia and Djibouti...this is a job for our clandestine people...they will resolve this from within...there are a hundred ways of doing this indirectly. I'm very fond of battles - with the enemies of course - with America and Israel, but *this* battle must be waged with judiciousness and calm."

Just a short time ago the American president honored Egyptian President Hosni Mubarak with a state dinner. Now she had forced him to resign and was coming to him. Morsi's assistant continued to whisper, "...there is talk of hundreds of millions of dollars from the Americans..."

Another grey haired man - this one without a tie - chimed in, "Even though this is a secret meeting we must all take an oath not to leak anything to the media..." after a quick interruption he replied, "OK... fine...the principles behind what I'm saying are not really secret...our war is with America and Israel not with Ethiopia..."

Just five months ago, Brothers had served as leaders, organizers and head-breakers for uprisings across the country. The flags of each mujahedeen group were carried. They had differences, of course, but they had all grown up on the *Protocols of the Elders of Zion*. They read, or had read to them, the writings of Sayyid Qutb and Hassan al-Banna...They were Brothers.

2.25

THE WHITE HOUSE
WASHINGTON,
DISTRICT OF COLUMBIA
1:55 P.M. 8 AUGUST 2011

President Winston cleared her throat and began speaking. "Good afternoon, everybody..." She looked around the room identifying friendly faces among the reporters present and moved forward with her prepared statement:

Last Friday, we learned that the United States received a downgrade by one of the credit rating agencies – not so much because they doubt our ability to pay our debt if we make good decisions, but because after witnessing a month of wrangling over raising the debt ceiling, they doubted our political system's ability to act. The markets, on the other hand, continue to believe our credit status is AAA. In fact, Warren Buffett, who knows a thing or two about good investments, said, "If there were a quadruple-A rating, I'd give the United States that." I, and most of the world's investors, agree.

That doesn't mean we don't have a problem. The fact is, we didn't need a rating agency to tell us that we need a balanced, long-term approach to deficit reduction. That was true last week. That was true last year. That was true the day I took office. And we didn't need a rating agency to tell us that the gridlock in Washington over the last several months has not been constructive, to say the least. We knew from the outset that a prolonged debate over the debt ceiling – a debate where the threat of default was used as a bargaining chip – could do enormous damage to our economy and the world's. That threat, coming after a string of economic disruptions in Europe, Japan and the Middle East, has now roiled the markets and dampened consumer confidence and slowed the pace of recovery.

So all of this is a legitimate source of concern. But here's the good news: Our problems are imminently solvable. And we know what we have to do to solve them. With respect to debt, our problem is not confidence in our credit – the markets continue to reaffirm our credit as among the world's safest. Our challenge is the need to tackle our deficits over the long term.

Last week, we reached an agreement that will make historic cuts to defense. The Affordable Care Act will reduce domestic spending. What we need to do now is combine those spending cuts with another step: tax reform that will ask those who can afford it to pay their fair share.

Making these reforms doesn't require any radical steps. What it does require is common sense and compromise. There are plenty of good ideas about how to achieve long-term deficit *reduction that doesn't hamper economic growth right now. The bipartisan fiscal commission that I set up put forth good proposals. The Senate's bipartisan Gang of Six came up with some good proposals. The Speaker and I came up with some good proposals when we came close to agreeing on a grand bargain.*

So it's not a lack of plans or policies that's the problem here. It's a lack of political will in Washington. It's the insistence on drawing lines in the sand, a refusal to put what's best for the country ahead of self-interest or party or ideology. And that's what we need to change.

I realize that after what we just went through, there's some skepticism that the so-called super committee… this joint committee that's been set up… will be able to reach a compromise, but my hope is that Friday's news will give us a renewed sense of urgency. I intend to present my own recommendations over the coming weeks on how we should proceed. And that committee will have this administration's full cooperation. And I assure you, we will stay on it until we get the job done.

Of course, as worrisome as the issues of debt and deficits may be, the most immediate concern of most Americans, and of concern to the marketplace as well, is the issue of jobs and the slow pace of recovery coming out of the worst recession in our lifetimes.

We should continue to make sure that if you're one of the millions of Americans who's out there looking for a job, you can get the unemployment insurance that your tax dollars contributed to. That will also put money in people's pockets and more customers in stores.

In fact, if Congress fails to extend the payroll tax cut and the unemployment insurance benefits that I've called for, it could mean one million fewer jobs and half a percent less growth. This is something we can do immediately, something we can do as soon as Congress gets back.

We should also help companies that want to repair our roads and bridges and airports, so that thousands of construction workers who've been without a job for the last few years can get a paycheck again. That will also help to spur economic growth.

These aren't Progressive proposals. These aren't big government proposals. These are all ideas that traditionally my opponents have agreed to, have agreed to countless times in the past. There's no reason we shouldn't act on them now. None.

I know we're going through a tough time right now. We've been going through a tough time for the last two and a half years. And I know a lot of people are worried about the future. But here's what I also know: There will always be economic factors that we can't control — earthquakes, spikes in oil prices, slowdowns in other parts of the world. But how we respond to those tests – that's entirely up to us.

Markets will rise and fall, but this is the United States of America. No matter what some agency may say, we've always been and always will be a AAA country. For all of the challenges we face, we continue to have the best universities, some of the most productive workers, the most innovative companies, the most adventurous entrepreneurs on Earth. What sets us apart is that we've always not just had the capacity, but also the will to act – the determination to shape our future; the willingness in our democracy to work out our differences in a sensible way and to move forward, not just for this generation but for the next generation.

And we're going to need to summon that spirit today. The American people have been through so much over the last few *years, dealing with the worst recession, the biggest financial crisis since the 1930s, and they've done it with grace. And they're working so hard to raise their families, and all they ask is that we work just as hard, here in this town, to make their lives a little easier. That's not too much to ask. And ultimately, the reason I am so hopeful about our future - the reason I have faith in these United States of America - is because of the American people. It's because of their perseverance, and their courage, and their willingness to shoulder the burdens we face… together, as one nation.*

One last thing. There is no one who embodies the qualities I mentioned more than the men and women of the United States Armed Forces. And this weekend, we lost 30 of them when their helicopter crashed during a mission in Afghanistan. And their loss is a stark reminder of the risks that our men and women in uniform take every single day on behalf of their county. Day after day, night after night, they carry out missions like this in the face of enemy fire and grave danger. And in this mission… as in so many others… they were also joined by Afghan troops, seven of whom lost their lives as well.

So I've spoken to our generals in the field, as well as President Karzai. And I know that our troops will continue the hard work of transitioning to a stronger Afghan government and ensuring that Afghanistan is not a safe haven for terrorists. We will press on. And we will succeed.

But now is also a time to reflect on those we lost, and the sacrifices of all who serve, as well as their families. These men and women put their lives on the line for the values that bind us together as a nation. They come from different places, and their backgrounds and beliefs reflect the rich diversity of America.

But no matter what differences they might have as individuals, they serve this nation as a team. They meet their responsibilities together. And some of them...like the 30 Americans who were lost this weekend... give their lives for their country. Our responsibility is to ensure that their legacy is an America that reflects their courage, their commitment, and their sense of common purpose. Thank you very much. God Bless America.

A few feet away, Hillary Barrett placed her government phone in her purse. She looked down at her personal, commercially encrypted phone and hit 'send'. She launched a text to Mr. Sludtsev... *W will need your help. Must move fast. Must be consequences for SP. If not managed others will downgrade. W will not be re-elected...* After 8, August 2011, Nikolay Sludtsev's allies never discussed the U.S. government's ability to repay its' debt in public again. Stories describing how manageable the U.S. government's interest payments could be bubbled to the surface in several friendly outlets.

2.26

ZUCCOTTI PARK

NEW YORK, NEW YORK

10:10 A.M.

17 SEPTEMBER 2011

Mohammad Mehrak edged cautiously into the crowd. Dispatch had told him to avoid the area because of the congestion, but he had parked his cab a few streets over and come on foot to see what was going on. He had only been in the United States for a couple of years and he was curious to see the event. Mohammad was not a large man. Growing up on a limited diet he was small compared to most of the Americans making up the crowd. He was inevitably bumped and jostled as he moved forward, but curiosity overpowered caution.

Up ahead he saw handmade signs. The first he read said "Wall Street is Our Street". The next said, "We Are the 99%". He pondered what it was intended to mean. On the surface it didn't seem profound, but nobody would go to the trouble of making it, coming here and carrying it if it didn't mean something *to them.*

A grimy bearded man wearing a wool hat pushed passed him muttering unintelligibly. Mohammad didn't take offense. This was scary, yes...but exhilarating. He could feel a life to the crowd itself. There was an energetic power from the congregation of hundreds of people in a confined space. He moved with the flow.

On his left, a tall stringy blond held out a paper cup in invitation. He accepted it and moved on as she held out another for the next person. It was a small cup of what looked like a heavily diluted unnaturally red juice. It might be cherry or strawberry flavoring. He wondered if it contained anything dangerous, but swept up in the moment, and thirsty, he downed it.

Up ahead he could hear chanting. He couldn't quite get the words, but as he flowed toward it, he could feel it. Its' rhythm felt good. He saw an attractive brown haired girl in a red tank top and inviting low-rise jeans flashing a sign that read, "None are more hopelessly enslaved than those who falsely believe they are free- Goethe". Wow. Now that *was* profound.

Mohammad thought back to why he left Iran. He had grown up poor - he and his mother subsisting on a meager government stipend. His father had been 'chosen' to serve as a martyr against Iraq. What this meant was that his father had been told that he would give his life for Allah in defense of Iran. He was given a cheap plastic key and told that it was the key to heaven. Before the soldiers came to take him, he had married his mother. Married men were not chosen as martyrs; but they told him he was coming anyway. They were unconcerned that she was already pregnant. Mohammad had never met his father. He understood that his father had charged into Iraqi machinegun fire in the fourth wave of unarmed teenagers with the bayonets of the Revolutionary Guards at his back. He had never met the man. He wondered if his father would be proud of him.

His mother died when he was 12. She became ill and never recovered. He had rummaged through her meager possessions for anything of value to salvage, and then he was on his own. He spoke and read English, and was intrigued by a book he found hidden under the foam pad she slept on. It was written by a man named Richard Maybury. It described the founding of America and the principles that historically guided the country. He had seen and heard the mullahs endless diatribes against the 'The Great Satan', but the book intrigued him. He couldn't help but notice that the government that had forced his father to commit suicide in the name of their earthly power games had claimed divine favoritism and insisted that the real evil on earth was a nation on the other side of the world founded on an ideology of liberty and limiting the power of man over other men.

Mohammad felt himself chanting with the crowd not knowing what he was saying, just matching their tone and intensity. On his right, he read a sign that read, "Let The US Days of Rage Begin."

The recently naturalized American paused and read another. "Capitalism doesn't work," He read,

"Redistribute Everything!" This made no sense to him. He saw a small flag waved with a red hammer and sickle on it. Were these people fools? They were clearly aware of the downside of overly powerful mega-corporations, but ignorant of the evils inherent in *any* form of government when combined with human nature. A *company* couldn't force anybody to do anything, but that *was* exactly the power withheld for governments. If you didn't like Apple, you didn't have to buy an iPhone. If you didn't like Walmart, you didn't have to work there. But when a government wanted you to do something, reason was only paper thin... then came coercion. That was the beauty of the United States. That was why he had risked everything to come here. Did these people not realize that the banks they were protesting were only relevant to their lives *after* they became tied to government, subsidized by government and had the weight of government thrown behind them? Were they really naïve enough to believe a government powerful enough to transform and enforce - simply manned by someone they liked - would please them?

Mohammad felt sick. He began to push back. The young man used every ounce of strength he had to swim toward a side street. This 'movement' would not include him.

2.27

THE WHITE HOUSE
WASHINGTON,
DISTRICT OF COLUMBIA
8:00 P.M.
22 NOVEMBER 2011

President Mallory Winston straightened herself and looked directly into the camera. She had memorized the first paragraph of her speech. She wanted to begin without focusing on her teleprompter:

Good evening. 10 years ago, America suffered the worst attack on our shores since Pearl Harbor. These killings were planned by Osama bin Laden and his al Qaeda network in Afghanistan, this was a new threat to our security - one in which the targets were no longer soldiers on a battlefield, but innocent men, women and children.

In the days that followed, our nation was united as we struck at al Qaeda and routed the Taliban in Afghanistan.

Then, our focus shifted. A second war was launched in Iraq, and we spent enormous blood and treasure to support a new government there. By the time I took office, the war in Afghanistan had entered its seventh year. But al Qaeda's leaders had escaped into Pakistan and were plotting new attacks, while the Taliban had regrouped and gone on the offensive. Without a new strategy and decisive action, our military commanders warned that we could face a resurgent al Qaeda, and a Taliban taking over large parts of Afghanistan.

For this reason, in one of the most difficult decisions that I've made as president, I ordered an additional 30,000 American troops into Afghanistan. Tonight, I can tell you that we are fulfilling that commitment. Thanks to our men and women in uniform, our civilian personnel, and our many coalition partners, we are meeting our goals. As a result, starting next month, we will be able to remove 10,000 of our troops from Afghanistan by the end of this year, and we will bring home a total of 33,000 troops by next summer. After this initial reduction, our troops will continue coming home at a steady pace as Afghan Security forces move into the lead. Our mission will change from combat to support. By 2014, this process of transition will be complete, and the Afghan people will be responsible for their own security.

Sergeant Ron Brown, a soldier with the 10th Mountain Division at Fort Drum, New York, watched the president's speech in on-base housing with his wife. A veteran of two deployments to Afghanistan, he couldn't contain himself. "You think there are Afghan troops that can 'take the lead'?!" He shouted at the television incredulously.

We are starting this drawdown from a position of strength. Al Qaeda is under more pressure than at any time since 9/11. Together with the Pakistanis, we have taken out more than half of al Qaeda's leadership, and I killed Osama bin Laden, the only leader that al Qaeda had ever known. This was a victory for all who have served since 9/11. We have put al Qaeda on a path to defeat, and we will not relent until the job is done.

CIA case officer Christine Englund watched the president on one of the screens at the Counter Terrorism Center in Langley, Virginia. "*You* killed bin Laden" she asked herself silently. "The Pakistani's 'helped' take out al Qaeda?" she groused thinking of the Pakistani intelligence officers captured with Taliban fighters. "Bin Laden is the only leader al Qaeda has ever known?"

In Afghanistan, we've inflicted serious losses on the Taliban and taken a number of its strongholds. Afghan Security Forces have grown by over 100,000 troops, and in some provinces and municipalities we have already begun to transition responsibility for security to the Afghan people. Of course, huge challenges remain. This is the beginning – but not the end – of our effort to wind down this war. We will have to do the hard work of keeping the gains that we have made, while we drawdown our forces and transition responsibility for security to the Afghan government. And next May, in Chicago, we will host a summit with our NATO allies and partners to shape the next phase of this transition.

Gunnery Sergeant Mike White, a member of the Marine Corps Pistol Team at Quantico, Virginia watched the president speaking on a laptop in the Weapons Training Battalion duty hut. "You're telling the bad guys when we're leaving?!" He bellowed to the small empty room. He knew that winning in Afghanistan was now an impossibility.

We do know that peace cannot come to a land that has known so much war without a political settlement. So as we strengthen the Afghan government and Security Forces, America will join initiatives that reconcile the Afghan people, including the Taliban. Our position on these talks is clear: they must be led by the Afghan government, and those who want to be a part of a peaceful Afghanistan must renounce violence, and abide by the Afghan Constitution.

Captain Jeremy Schneider, a chaplain at Fort Benning, Georgia quietly spoke to the television in a busy Atlanta International Airport terminal. He said, "Don't you know that the Afghan Constitution is sha-riah based? There will be neither peace nor freedom for anyone." Passengers flowed past without taking notice.

The goal that we seek is achievable, and can be expressed simply: no safe-haven from which al Qaeda or its affiliates can launch attacks against our homeland, or our allies. We will not try to make Afghanistan a perfect place. We will not police its streets or patrol its mountains indefinitely. That is the responsibility of the Afghan government, which must step up its ability to protect its people; and move from an economy shaped by war to one that can sustain a lasting peace. What we can do, and will do, is build a partnership with the Afghan people that endures – one that ensures that we will be able to continue targeting terrorists and supporting a sovereign Afghan government.

My fellow Americans, this has been a difficult decade for our country. We have learned anew the profound cost of war – a cost that has been paid by the nearly 4,500 Americans who have given their lives in Iraq, and the over 1,500 who have done so in Afghanistan – men and women who will not live to enjoy the freedom that they defended. Thousands more have been wounded. Some have lost limbs on the field of battle, and others still battle the demons that have followed them home. Yet tonight, we take comfort in knowing that the tide of war is receding. We have ended our combat mission in Iraq, with 100,000 American troops already out of that country. And even as there will be dark days ahead in Afghanistan, the light of a secure peace can be seen in the distance. These long wars will come to a responsible end.

We must chart a more centered course. Like generations before, we must embrace America's singular role in the course of human events. But we must be as pragmatic as we are passionate; as strategic as we are resolute. When innocents are being slaughtered and global security endangered, we don't have to choose between standing idly by or acting on our own. Instead, we must rally international action, which we are doing in Libya, protecting the Libyan people and giving them the chance to determine their destiny.

We are all a part of one American family. Though we have known disagreement and division, we are bound together by the creed that is written into our founding documents, and a conviction that the United States of America is a country that

can achieve whatever it sets out to accomplish. Now, let us fin-
ish the work at hand. Let us responsibly end these wars, and
reclaim the American Dream that is at the center of our story.
May God bless the United States of America.

President Winston took a long, silent look into the
camera. She ended the session and stepped away from
her position. She was pleased with her performance.

2.28

OGAWA PLAZA

OAKLAND, CALIFORNIA

11:30 A.M. 1 MARCH 2012

Jon Greer sat looking out the window of a chartered bus wondering how he had gotten to this point in his life. Not too long ago, he sold cars for a living. He went to work clean shaven in khakis wearing a different color button down shirt each day. That seemed like a life time ago. Then the economy went bad, and here he was - bearded, uncut hair, living on the streets. His last shower was from a section of garden hose attached to a water spicket behind a liquor store. His last meal came from a garbage dumpster behind an In-N-Out Burger. The new Jon seemed like a completely different person from the old Jon.

His head pressed against the glass leaving a grease mark where it rolled back and forth. Deep in thought, the streets and buildings gliding by outside didn't register. He thought how glad he was that he didn't have a wife or kids. He pondered how weird it was that his first reason was the shame he would feel from them seeing him jobless and living like this. The practicality of not being able to support them only provided a secondary reason.

His introspection ended as the bus cornered, making whining sounds and choppily came to a stop. He looked to the man seated next to the door for instructions. That was the man that paid him $20 to get on the bus… however many… hours ago. He had gotten on with a group of six other street people that he did not know. Each had received the same. After only a few stops, the bus had been filled. He was curious if what the man had told them was true, but desperation and monotony rendered fear and caution flavorless.

The man stepped out the door as soon as it opened and spoke privately with a short heavy set black lady that seemed to be expecting him. She wore a fluorescent yellow t-shirt with some kind of union logo on it. After a few moments, the woman stepped onto the bus and said, "Thank you for volunteering to do this important job. When you file off the bus you will be given the sandwich Steve promised you…" Jon could see a Subaru backed up with the rear hatch open and a tall stack of Subway sandwiches inside. There was a vat of what might be coffee and Styrofoam cups next to it.

"…once you have your sandwich and your sign, Micah will lead you to the jobsite. He will show you where to meet to get your dinner and another $20 tonight…" the woman concluded happily. Her tone made him think she must have been a school teacher at some point. When she finished and got off the bus, he stood and filed off with the others.

He was handed a folded sign. He opened it and looked at it as he moved toward the sandwich line. It was hand-written in bold red capital letters…"SEIZE THE BANKS". Ok, he thought. All and all, he was pleased that this was pretty close to what he was told they were getting into. Living on the streets had made him paranoid, though he didn't think you could call it paranoia when there were so many good reasons to be cautious. He had seen every type of assault imaginable in the past months, he thought.

Jon, tucked the re-folded sign in his armpit and gratefully accepted a sandwich and a cup of coffee with his free hands. He looked to find Micah as he had been told to do.

Micah was easy to pick out. He was wearing the same fluorescent yellow union t-shirt that 'Weezie' - he named her in his mind for her resemblance to an old sitcom character he had seen - was wearing. Micah was close by and attentive. It was clear they were not going to let anybody get lost.

Micah led the single file line across Clay Street and down 16th. He looked back and saw a burly look-ing man in the same yellow t-shirt bringing up the rear of their formation. Jon wondered who had paid for all of this. Was it the union? The thought left his mind as Micah stopped. They were about to turn right into a public plaza, but before they came into view, Micah stopped and turned to them. "We will be watching on the news. Whichever of you we see on camera will get

100$..." Micah asked if anyone needed to be reminded where they were to meet up later, then re-explained the information after nobody asked for it.

Micah stood and collected their empty cups and wrappers in a garbage bag as the line filed past. Jon didn't give him the sandwich wrapper as the others did, though. He decided to save part of his B.M.T. for later. He re-wrapped it and sealed it with the sticker that had been on it before putting it away in his pocket. The sticker read: "From your friends at the Free Community Partnership".

Jon turned the corner into Ogawa Plaza and could see that they were joining a large crowd. He began reading each of the signs that he could see. The first one said, "Occupy Everything".

2.29

THE WHITE HOUSE WASHINGTON, DISTRICT OF COLUMBIA 6:30 P.M. 16 MARCH 2012

President Mallory Winston turned the page on the table in front of her and looked up at the man speaking. Thomas Deering was explaining how "Mallorycare" would improve all aspects of the lives of the people living in America to the table of bureaucrats that had been invited to the White House. Mallory Winston new that the public would fear change and she knew that Congress resented what they considered her imperial attitude and would feel the need to posture in opposition to implementing the Affordable Care Act. She also knew that the aggressiveness of implementation of the Act would be in the hands of a network of unelected officials. If she could build an alliance with those in a position to make it happen, she could get what she wanted - regardless of the opposition.

"Preventive Medicine." He continued with a dramatic pause. "we all know that an ounce of prevention is worth a pound of cure…" he looked around the table "…just think of the Preventive Medicine that can be provided for the good of the people when the Affordable Care Act is fully implemented."

"We will have a base line for health care. The son of a single undocumented immigrant mother will be afforded the same care as a rich business owner. Wall Street fat cats will be penalized with real bite when they attempt to obtain superior care for their own children. Nobody will be without protection and there will be strong disincentives to prevent obtaining what others don't have…you all…I am sure are familiar with the broad strokes…but I want you to project yourself into the future and consider what *you* can do to make America a more fair country, and *finally*, a good neighbor in the global community."

He looked at a chubby woman wearing thick glasses at the far end of the table; "Marilyn, with the amount of federal subsidies flowing into the Act's programs, how hard do you think it will be for you to implement nutritional standards for the health of the people? Do you think you could inhibit the ability of vendors to provide the foods we know to be unhealthy when we are each responsible for providing our brothers' and sisters' health care?"

"Curtiss" he said to an impeccably dressed man with blonde highlights "What do you think could be done to limit the pollution the people ingest from fossil fuels?

Do you think clean energy - regardless of the so-called cost - could be made more palatable when we are each responsible for the medical care of our fellow humans?"

"Stacy" Deering barked "How apt to make racist, sexist, homophobic hate speech fueled remarks is a man whose treatments for herpes may or may not be publicly accessible information?" Deering said indelicately. "How likely are we to hear one of those housewife soccer mom's whine about the new curriculum her 'little angels' are being exposed to at school when she knows that her miscarriage of 'unknown cause' is in the central record *safe guarded* from her nosy relatives?"

"John..." he said to a bearded pot-bellied man with a miniature ATF badge lapel pin on his collar "When we have commissioned a hundred studies to demonstrate the health hazard that firearms pose, how much opposition can be eroded from those gun-nuts? When the people see statistic after statistic from medical doctors opposed to gun carnage, how many dollars will the NRA be able to muster to pour into the 'cowboy coalition'?"

"Janet..." a stout woman in glasses perked up "what are the health repercussions of the racist's attempts to keep immigrants from crossing our borders? And Frank? Frank... what happens when union membership correlates with documentable health benefit? Just... *maybe...* we can grow the unions? What do you think?"

"What do you all think?" Thomas Deering queried with passion in his voice. "I encourage you to consider what you personally can do to make America better. Picture yourself behind the director's desk of your respective agencies. Picture yourself years from now looking back at the impact *you* had on American Progress. Was the hard work not worth it? Is it not worth sticking your neck out to help Mallory Winston? Could you live with yourself if you aided those fascist, sexist enemies of progress…" he roared, then continued quietly "…Or if you just did nothing but the narrow *minimum* of your job?" Deering had them on the edge of their seats. There was a reason Thomas was the neuro-linguistic programming specialist Hillary Barrett had brought in to lead these sessions.

As the group was filing out – young agency executives giddy from the prestige of having been in their first conference with The President (and at far more junior positions than normally rated such attention) Mallory Winston motioned for one efficient looking, short-haired woman to stop.

Deputy Commissioner of Internal Revenue, Lucille Turner was no stranger to the White House. Unlike the others, she had been here more than 100 times before over the past two years. "Lucille…I just want you to know how much I value your important work. As you know, when The Affordable Care Act is implemented, I want your agency to take the lead in enforcement. You will have to modernize and grow, of course…" she said looking away and speaking of the agency as if she were speaking of Lucille herself. "And *when* I'm re-elected… *if* I'm re-elected…" she said uncharacteristically, "…I want you heading it up…" Mallory Winston said with a wink confirming what Lucille had long believed.

3.

NUCLEAR SECURITY SUMMIT

SEOUL, SOUTH KOREA

2:30 P.M.

26 MARCH 2012

Russian President Dmitri Medvedev walked down a private corridor continuing his discussion with President Mallory Winston. "…Mr. Putin is anxious to know if he can count on you to help rescue our environment?" he asked earnestly, referencing the man who had gone from being the Russian President to being the Prime Minister.

"…I just can't deliver a carbon tax under our system…" President Winston stated. She was referring to a wide range of proposed taxes designed to provide disincentives to people that used carbon based fuels. It was taken as an item of faith among environmental activists that reducing carbon dioxide - the gas given off by humans and consumed by plants - would be beneficial for the earth's environment. The concept was based on the idea that carbon dioxide caused 'global warming' and that man's production of carbon dioxide was a significant part of that equation.

"...I understand..." Medvedev consoled. There were proportionally small numbers of zealots that supported this idea. There were key bureaucrats whose fiefdoms were expanded when they found elements of the 'green' programs they could support, and there were academics whose livelihood came from climate change related grants. But United States citizens ranged from hostile to indifferent regarding 'climate change' programs. Everyone loved the environment and was proud of how well the United States had cleaned up pollution in the last 30 years, but they also understood that the new programs advocated were sufficiently costly that they would dramatically decrease their productivity and crash their standard of living regardless of how nicely they were packaged by any politician.

"...Vladimir knows I have wanted this from long before *he* ever got serious about the climate..." President Winston crowed. "...but Americans cannot be convinced. They are going to have to be pushed from the outside...the international... *pressure*...we discussed will be the only way..."

Medvedev replied, "...Mr. Putin instructed me to inform you that you can depend on the United Nations' support in this...he personally guarantees that he will do his part."

"...Of course you know Mr. Putin cannot provide for the security of *our* people if America supports a missile defense shield for Europe...this would alter the balance of power...and destabilize the region..." Medvedev tied a second thread to the American 'climate change' initiative. All the while the man found it amazing that Europeans and Americans would even consider such radical claims without scientific proof. The idea of such catastrophically costly regulation based on this nonsense was deliciously bizarre. The fact that Western reporting used the statement "scientists have come to consensus that global warming is a fact" was insane. The scientific method depends upon hypothesizing, making predictions based upon the hypothesis, and experimentation that either confirms or refutes the hypothesis. Making a point based on the claim that 'scientists' had achieved 'consensus' was an appeal to authority. This reasoning was in and of itself a violation *of* the scientific method. It was an anti-scientific claim.

The idea that a giant potato shaped mass of rock, soil, water and air moving through space and orbiting a sun would have a climate without variation was beyond belief. The idea that even *all* of man's productivity combined would be enough to significantly alter these variations was... *a guess.* And the assumption that somehow freezing the status of the world's climate in place would for some reason be 'good' was beyond comprehension.

Mallory Winston and Dmitri Medvedev emerged through a side door into a media room, glided into their respective seats and wrapped up their conversation before the microphones were turned on.

The American President said "...This is my last election. After my election I have more flexibility..."

"...I understand. I will transmit this information to Vladimir..." the Russian President replied.

3.1

GRAND HYATT, ROOSEVELT BALLROOM WASHINGTON, DISTRICT OF COLUMBIA 10:10 A.M. 10 MAY 2012

"**...L**ucille, a few months ago there were some concerns about the IRS's review of 501(c)(4) organizations, of applications from pro-Constitution and Bill of Rights organizations," Martin Stout, a veteran tax lawyer, asked Deputy Commissioner of Internal Revenue Lucille Turner using a microphone he was provided. She had just wrapped up her speech and finished giving what people understood to be her prepared remarks. "I was just wondering if you could provide an update," Stout asked from within the crowd.

Lucille Turner glanced briefly at the soothing blue color of her dress' sleeve, quickly ran her fingers through the side of her short Auburn hair and replied matter-of-factly: "We get about 60,000 applications for tax exemption every year, most of them are 501(c)(3) organizations. But between 2010 and 2012 we started seeing a very big uptick in the number of 501(c)(4) applications we were receiving and many of these organizations applying more than doubled, about 1500 in 2010 and over 3400 in 2012. So we saw a big increase in these kind of applications, many of which indicated that they were going to be involved in advocacy work." She paused and continued:

So our line people in Cincinnati who handled the applications did what we call centralization of these cases. They centralized work on these in one particular group. They do that for efficiency and consistency- something we do whenever we see an uptick in a new kind of application or something we haven't seen before. Folks might remember from back a few years ago we had credit counseling organizations and we centralized those cases. We had mortgage foreclosure cases and we centralized those cases. We do it for consistency. So they went ahead and did that. How they do centralization is... they have a list in their office that they give out to folks who are screening cases that says if it is one of these kind of cases and it can't be screened it needs to go to group X. So centralization was perfectly fine.

However, in these cases, the way they did the centralization was not so fine. Instead of referring to the cases as advocacy cases, they actually used case names on this list. They used names like 'Constitution' or 'Patriots' and they selected cases simply because the applications had those names in the title. That was wrong, that was absolutely incorrect, insensitive, and inappropriate - that's not how we go about selecting cases for further review. We don't select for review because they have a particular name.

The other thing that happened was they also, in some cases, cases sat around for a while. They also sent some letters out that were far too broad, asking questions of these organizations that weren't really necessary for the type of application. In some cases you probably read that they asked for contributor names. That's not appropriate, not usual, there are some very limited times when we might need that but in most of these cases where they were asked they didn't do it correctly and they didn't do it with a higher level of review. As I said, some of them sat around for too long."

Turner continued, "What have we done to take care of this?" She glanced down at her notes and continued, "Oh, let me back up…They didn't do this because of any political bias." She said quickly bringing her eyes back up when she caught herself glancing to the ground. "They did it because they were working together. This was a streamlined way for them to refer to the cases." She said avoiding eye contact with any single set of eyes in the crowd.

They didn't have the appropriate level of sensitivity about how this might appear to others and it was just wrong. So when we found out about it we did a couple of things. First, we said that list that goes around for centralizing cases - any changes on that list have to be reviewed and approved at the Director of Rulings & Agreements level - so line staff can no longer change or add to that list without calling us to look at it.

We also went back and looked at questions that had been sent out to folks because some of them were extensive and where the questions weren't necessary we gave the organizations flex-ibility as to which questions they needed to answer and gave them more time to answer them. In some cases we told them to just ignore the letter we already sent and sent a new list of questions. In some cases, we said we don't need those questions answered...We can deal with your application without responses to those questions. We also sorted the cases to try and figure out which cases needed a further look and which cases could be handled through...almost a screening process. We might need a little bit more information.

"The problem in the (c)(4) area is that the kind of activity the organizations were doing is okay for (c)(4) s but it can't be their primary activity. So that weighing and balancing is a little different than when we have a (c)(3) that says you can't do any political activity. That's a pretty easy question. So I guess my bottom line here is that we at the IRS should apologize for that, it was not intentional," Turner stifled a facial tick at the edge of her lip, but continued without pause "...and as soon as we found out what was going on, we took steps to make it better and I don't expect that to reoccur."

She continued, speaking evenly now, "As long as we are on the topic of potential political activity, it's a good time to remind all of you as you are looking at filing for 2012 there was a lot of political activity in organizations this past year and so we'll be looking at the 527(f) tax, as we see the 2012 990s coming in, so make sure that your clients are appropriately computing the 527(f) tax."

Deputy Commissioner Turner, looked at her old friend Martin Stout without betraying the gratitude she felt for asking the question she had previously requested that he ask. An IRS Inspector General's report was going to be announced - maybe in as soon as a week - but now nobody could ever say that Lucille Turner was not the first to publicly report the wrong-doing that occurred under her supervision. She was involved in a dangerous game, but her fear subsided as the likelihood of criminal prosecution was blunted. She was a little surprised at the breathlessness of the reporters present.

One that she had observed dozing earlier was now alert and full of energy. "Are you saying that the IRS stonewalled applications from groups critical of President Winston and her policies?" he asked. She felt her face flush red. *Shit!* That *was* pointed.

"I can't answer any questions, I have to go now…" and the Deputy Commissioner turned on her heel, and strode from behind the podium tugging at the over-sized navy blue beads around her neck.

3.2

SUPREME COURT BUILDING WASHINGTON, DISTRICT OF COLUMBIA 10:10 A.M. 27 JUNE 2012

The 18th Chief Justice of the United States, Wilson Conrad, sat behind his MacBook Pro studying the screen through his half lens reading glasses. The notebook device wasn't his government computer, but like anyone senior enough to get away with it, he preferred to work on his own equipment. This practice gave greater privacy from auditors and anyone else who might invade his privacy and it helped him to circumvent some of the juvenile firewalls set up for government systems.

He scrolled down through the document he had been working on. It was the culmination of a great deal of work and it would command people's attention for decades. It was the majority opinion for Alliance of

Business and Commerce, et al. v. Secretary of Health and Human Services, et al... It would be the verdict for the case determining the constitutionality of 'Mallorycare.'

"...The Court today finds the statute's requirement with penalties for non-compliance to be beyond the authority granted the enacting body. The argument that the mandated citizen purchases are instead options subject to a tax is without merit..." Conrad read with pride. He had witnessed the President state explicitly that Mallorycare was not a tax. It was a little late for her team to now argue that it *was* a tax in order to find a loophole of legal justification for this blatant power grab.

...The Court regards the statute as a debilitated, inoperable version of health-care regulation that Congress did not enact and the public does not expect. It makes enactment of sensible health-care regulation more difficult, since Congress cannot start afresh but must take as its point of departure a jumble of now senseless provisions... And it leaves the public and the States to expend vast sums of money on requirements that may or may not survive the necessary congressional revision...

...Holding that the Individual Mandate is a tax would be entirely unsupported by the Constitution. A judgment supporting the statute in contradiction of legal status would usher in new federalism concerns and place an unaccustomed strain upon the Union. Those States that decline participation would be required to subsidize, by the federal tax dollars taken from their citizens, vast grants to the States that accept the Expansion. If that destabilizing political dynamic, so antagonistic to a harmonious Union, is to be introduced at all, it must be by Congress, not by the Judiciary.

...The Constitution, though it dates from the founding of the Republic, has powerful meaning and vital relevance to our own times. The constitutional protections that this case involves are protections of Structure - structural protections—notably, the restraints imposed by federalism and separation of powers. It is the responsibility of the Court to teach otherwise, to remind our people that the Framers considered structural protections of freedom the most important ones, for which reason they alone were embodied in the original Constitution and not left to later amendment. The fragmentation of power produced by the structure of our Government is central to liberty, and when we destroy it, we place liberty at peril. Today's decision vindicates this truth...

Chief Justice Conrad hastily scanned down to the final sentence: "...For the reasons here stated, we find the Act invalid in its entirety." This was going to create a hell of a rift with the Executive branch, but there was no other choice. The Act didn't overstep constitutionally imposed limitations on the power of government over individual citizens, it simply pretended that there were none.

Conrad rubbed his eyes, and wanting a break and a moment's reflection before forwarding the document back to the four other justices providing the verdict of the majority he turned his focus to the window containing one of his personal email accounts and expanded it.

The top email, having just arrived, was from a favorite site and carried the header, "Tera Patrick is thinking of you, Wilson." How weird. Tera Patrick was his favorite actress, and the personalization of spam like this certainly caught his attention. In fact, it was a little odd. He never used his true name or personal email accounts on adult websites.

In a second he was inside the email, looking at a picture of a part-Asian, part-Anglo beauty that bore a striking resemblance to Tera. Dread filled him immediately as he clicked the link and was delivered to the destination site. It looked just like his favorite adult site, but the video displayed most prominently was not Tera Patrick. He did not know that the page had been created just for him and that there were no other routes to it outside the link he had been provided. He felt empty and sick. He knew what was coming. He *knew* Ms. Patrick's doppelgänger. He pressed 'play' wishing the earth would swallow him up.

He watched a video of his pale, nude, corpulent, middle aged body fucking 'Tera.' He felt revulsion. His wife was going to hate him. The *world* was going to hate him. He was going to lose his entire life, and he looked like a pathetic caricature of a *real* porn actor. He knew how it ended, but when he watched the end of his performance and the moment when he disappeared into the shower to clean himself up, he saw the real finale'. Beautiful, disheveled 'Tera', still braided and wearing the socks from her schoolgirl outfit moved a newspaper aside revealing a Hawaii driver's license. On the day the video was shot, she was 16 years old.

There was no way... There was just *no* way. He read the one comment posted beneath his video. It said, "The Act stands. Join the minority. Deliver the verdict tomorrow."

3.3

THE WHITE HOUSE
WASHINGTON,
DISTRICT OF COLUMBIA
8:05 P.M.
20 AUGUST 2012

President Mallory Winston looked up at the camera and began speaking earnestly, "My fellow Americans, tonight I want to talk to you about Syria, why it matters and where we go from here." There were no reporters present. There would be no questions taken:

Over the past two years, what began as a series of peaceful protests against the oppressive Bashar al-Assad regime has turned into a brutal civil war. More than 100,000 people have been killed. Millions have fled the country. In that time, America has worked with allies to provide humanitarian support, to help the moderate opposition, and to shape a political settlement, but I have resisted calls for military action because we cannot resolve someone else's civil war through force, particularly after a decade of war in Iraq and Afghanistan.

Recently, chemical weapons were used in Syria. The world saw thousands of videos, cell phone pictures, and social media accounts from the attack, and humanitarian organizations told stories of hospitals packed with people who had symptoms of poison gas.

Moreover, we know the Assad regime was responsible. In the days leading up to the attacks, we know that Assad's chemical weapons personnel prepared for an attack near an area where they mix sarin gas. They distributed gas masks to their troops. Then they fired rockets from a regime-controlled area into 11 neighborhoods that the regime has been trying to wipe clear of opposition forces. Shortly after those rockets landed, the gas spread, and hospitals filled with the dying and the wounded.

We know senior figures in Assad's military machine reviewed the results of the attack and the regime increased their shelling of the same neighborhoods in the days that followed. We've also studied samples of blood and hair from people at the site that tested positive for sarin. When dictators commit atrocities, they depend upon the world to look the other way until those horrifying pictures fade from memory, but the facts cannot be denied.

The question now is what the United States of America and the international community is prepared to do about it, because what happened to those people - to those children - is not only a violation of international law, it's also a danger to our security. Let me explain why. If fighting spills beyond Syria's borders, these weapons could threaten allies like Turkey, Jordan and Israel.

Captain Jason Abernathy, a cavalry soldier at Fort Hood, Texas, watching the speech on television asked himself why the president didn't mention Iraq. As a veteran of three Iraq deployments, he knew that droves of Sunni terrorists from al Qaeda and the other groups crossed the Syria/Iraq border at will. He also knew that whatever side the United States intervened on, there would be generations of enemies created.

This is not a world we should accept. This is what's at stake. And that is why, after careful deliberation, I determined that it is in the national security interests of the United States to respond to the Assad regime's use of chemical weapons through a targeted military strike. The purpose of this strike would be to deter Assad from using chemical weapons, to degrade his regime's ability to use them, and to make clear to the world that we will not tolerate their use.

That's my judgment as commander-in-chief, but I'm also the president of the world's oldest constitutional democracy. So even though I possess the authority to order military strikes, I believed it was right in the absence of a direct or imminent threat to our security to take this debate to Congress.

Technical Sergeant Janine Lindsky, an aviation ordnance specialist at Patrick Air Force Base in Florida watched President Winston on the television in her temporary quarters. She found herself wondering why the hell didn't the president give a damn about congress when she kicked the top off another ant hill by firing cruise missiles into Libya? Worse still, the president *did* seek the approval of the United Nations, setting a ridiculous precedent.

Now, I know that after the terrible toll of Iraq and Afghanistan, the idea of any military action - no matter how limited - is not going to be popular. After all, I've spent four-and-a-half years ending wars, not starting them. Our troops are out of Iraq. Our troops are coming home from Afghanistan. And I know Americans want all of us in Washington - especially me - to concentrate on the task of building our nation here at home.

So let me answer some of the most important questions that I've heard from members of Congress and that I've read in letters that you've sent to me. First, many of you have asked, won't this put us on a slippery slope to another war? One man wrote to me this nation is sick and tired of war.

My answer is simple. I will not put American boots on the ground in Syria. I will not pursue an open-ended action like Iraq or Afghanistan. I will not pursue a prolonged air campaign like Libya or Kosovo. This engagement will not include 'decisive' action.

Master Chief Rodney Brown, a shore patrol officer at the Naval Amphibious Base at Little Creek, Virginia yelled at the television in his duty hut. "The moment you attack a country or anyone in it, you are at war!" Did this president really not understand that? What idiot would be convinced to go to war by a promise not to win it?

Others have asked whether it's worth acting if we don't take out Assad. Now, some members of Congress have said there's no point in simply doing a pinprick strike in Syria. Let me make something clear: The United States military doesn't do pinpricks. Even a limited strike will send a message to Assad that no other nation can deliver.

I don't think we should remove another dictator with force. We learned from Iraq and Libya that doing so makes us responsible for all that comes next. But a targeted strike can make Assad - or any other dictator - think twice before using chemical weapons.

Many of you have asked a broader question: Why should we get involved at all in a place that's so complicated and where, as one person wrote to me, those who come after Assad may be enemies of human rights?

It's true that some of Assad's opponents are extremists. But al Qaeda will only draw strength in a more chaotic Syria if people there see the world doing nothing to prevent innocent civilians from being gassed to death.

Special Agent Donald Jackson watched President Winston's speech on a cable news channel in the FBI's Washington Field Office. "Am I the only person that sees what nonsense this is?" he asked himself. Assad was a long-time terrorist sponsoring thug, but his opposition was a conglomeration of Islamic supremacist militias. It was a certainty that the most vicious of them would come out holding the reins of power if he were toppled.

The majority of the Syrian people, and the Syrian opposition we work with, just want to live in peace, with dignity and freedom. And the day after any military action, we would redouble our efforts to achieve a political solution that strengthens those who reject the forces of tyranny and extremism.

Over the last few days, we've seen some encouraging signs, in part because of the credible threat of U.S. military action, as well as constructive talks that I had with President Putin. The Russian government has indicated a willingness to join with the international community in pushing Assad to give up his chemical weapons. The Assad regime has now admitted that it has these weapons and even said they'd join the Chemical Weapons Convention, which prohibits their use.

It's too early to tell whether this offer will succeed, and any agreement must verify that the Assad regime keeps its commitments, but this initiative has the potential to remove the threat of chemical weapons without the use of force, particularly because Russia is one of Assad's strongest allies.

I have therefore asked the leaders of Congress to postpone a vote to authorize the use of force while we pursue this diplomatic path. I'm sending my Secretary of State to meet his Russian counterpart on Thursday, and I will continue my own discussions with President Putin.

I've spoken to the leaders of two of our closest allies – France and the United Kingdom – and we will work together in consultation with Russia and China to put forward a resolution at the U.N. Security Council requiring Assad to give up his chemical weapons and to ultimately destroy them under international control. We'll also give U.N. inspectors the opportunity to report their findings about what happened on August 21st, and we will continue to rally support from allies from Europe to the Americas, from Asia to the Middle East, who agree on the need for action.

I'd ask every member of Congress and those of you watching at home tonight to view those videos of the attack, and then ask, what kind of world will we live in if the United States of

America sees a dictator brazenly violate international law with poison gas and we choose to look the other way?

Franklin Roosevelt once said, "Our national determination to keep free of foreign wars and foreign entanglements cannot prevent us from feeling deep concern when ideas and principles that we have cherished are challenged." Our ideals and principles, as well as our national security, are at stake in Syria, along with our leadership of a world where we seek to ensure that the worst weapons will never be used. America is not the world's policeman, but when modest effort and risk can stop children from being gassed to death I believe we should act.

Thank you, God bless the United States of America.

Mallory Winston ended her speech and looked away from the camera as she turned to depart. Her chief of staff for re-election gave her an enthusiastic thumbs-up from the back of the room. The President strode out of the room feeling confident.

3.4

WALL STREET

NEW YORK, NEW YORK

7:00 P.M.

10 SEPTEMBER 2012

Hillary Barrett was at the end of her report before Nikolay Sludtsev interrupted with anything other than questions for clarification and requests for additional details. Hillary had a regular appointment with Mr. Sludtsev to keep him appraised of President Winston's activities. They preferred face-to-face meetings to avoid creating 'controversial' paper trails and potentially embarrassing electronic records of their conversations. They met after routine staff members had already departed for the day and they left their smart phones in a special safe in the Magna- Stellar Fund's receiving room when meeting at Sludtsev's fund offices. The offices were regularly swept for listening devices and they did not speak freely in the rooms with Internet-linked computers in them.

Hillary Barrett finished briefing her old 'boss' and then Sludtsev delivered his own short monologue. This was how he sensitized Barrett to his interests. He also had a need to let her know some of his latest initiatives so that she could either support them accordingly or be cautious not to contradict them.

"…Hillary, there is something else you must be aware of…" Sludtsev continued in his business-professional tone "…'Occupy' has served its purpose." He looked down his list and began to summarize…"As you know, we had to counter the 'TEA Party'…"

Sludtsev referred to a popular American movement that called itself the TEA Party. It was an homage to the Boston Tea Party where Americans surreptitiously dumped British shipments of Tea into Boston Harbor at the outset of the Revolutionary War. It was the origin of the 'no taxation without representation' ideal. The 2010 TEA Party claimed to be "Taxed Enough Already". They weren't a singular group, just a collection of individuals and groups that had a strong conviction that the United States government should not be permitted to spend money it had to borrow, that it should not be permitted to raise more taxes and that the country would be best served by defunding a wide range of programs not supported by the U.S. Constitution. Sludtsev saw them as fools. They obviously didn't understand that the moment the United States ended the gold standard for the dollar, the U.S. government collected taxes from the world. The Federal Reserve simply had more dollars printed and digitally created thereby invisibly taxing anyone that did business in dollars – the whole world - on one level or another.

Regardless of their myopic view and intellectual short comings, their ideas tapped a widely felt sentiment that looked like a spark hitting a dried forest. In 2010, The Progressive National Committee had entered the mid-term elections with the first woman president ever elected in the United States. Voters were proud to have proven how modern they were. The PNC had strong majorities in the House of Representatives and the Senate. They were positioned to place judges in the Supreme Court that did not see close adherence to the Constitution's Bill of Rights as necessary in the modern world. After the 2008 financial disaster on Wall Street, voters had permitted the President they had faith in to nationalize banks, auto manufacturers and other industries that needed guidance.

But by 2010, reality had set in. The President needed qualifications beyond being a woman. Nationalization of industries was not having a beneficial effect. Central planning did not work any better in America than it did in Cuba, Russia or anywhere else. Voters were not entirely unaware that hand-picked government economic numbers were anemically optimistic each month, but revised down immediately before the new month's 'optimistic' numbers were reported. The PNC lost The House in a landslide. They very nearly lost the Senate, and polls suggested that if there was a presidential election, Mallory Winston would have lost as well.

The bottom line was that the TEA Party - while not a single group - represented a widely popular appeal to the old fashioned ideals of self-sufficiency within a free market and limits on the size, cost and power of government.

It had taken a lot to re-cast protesting government deficit spending and the unilateral presidential expansion of powers as a modern Ku Klux Klan, but it had been done. The Free Community Partnership had to pull every lever it had, but it had been necessary. TEA party protests at IRS buildings were reported as hundreds when, in fact, there were thousands. At a rally with more than a thousand present, Sludtsev's people searched endlessly for the use of a racist word that could be televised. This grass roots political problem had to be shut down before it ignited the forest and Sludtsev had made that one of his people's top three priorities.

Not only did he pin his hopes on de-legitimizing the crowds that opposed his initiatives and the politician's that carried them forward, but he understood that there had to be a counter-message. This was basic tradecraft for the KGB officers that had tutored him over the years.

"...Polling data all shows that our efforts were successful. The Tea Party name is significantly less palatable to voters than it was before we began our initiatives. They will be under control for 2012. But there is something else..." Sludtsev continued "...voters have an extremely negative view of the 'Occupy' protesters."

Sludtsev had thrown his weight behind 'Occupy'. Where there were 100 protesters present he had articles published describing 1000's. Where there were riots, he had news stories discussing activism, but unfortunately, unable to obtain footage of the event accept for the victims of police pepper spray afterward. His people had done their best to grow crowds where it might be of help and to put the best face on the patchwork of individuals brought together to protest. These initiatives served their purpose. Where the TEA Party that criticized Mallory Winston's policies were now sexists and racists according to popular culture, the 'Occupy' group claimed ownership of 'diversity' – all the while advancing the idea that the corporate corruption they despised could only be curtailed if the government was granted wider powers.

"…I am withdrawing my support from Occupy. Tell Mallory not to publicly mention them again."

3.5

THE WHITE HOUSE WASHINGTON, DISTRICT OF COLUMBIA 6:50 P.M. 22 OCTOBER 2012

Sergeant Angel Rodriguez stepped into the "Marine Room" and carefully pulled the door shut behind him. As soon as he saw what Sergeant Johnson was watching on the television he let out a bellow.

"Bro...you're watching the communist propaganda network?!" he said with disgust referring to one of the cable news networks widely known for 'slanting' their reporting. Rodriguez had been in a heavy firefight with insurgents in Fallujah, and had three brothers hit by machinegun fire and RPG shrapnel before their FAC (forward air controller) ended the fight with a well-placed air-strike. The network Johnson was watching right now had reported that "Marines *claiming* to receive *sniper* fire bombed a mosque and killed 18 worshipping Muslims." Almost every combat Marine had a similar story.

He placed his immaculate white dress blue cover in his cubby hole on the wall, quickly insured the gold eagle, globe and anchor device was perfectly straight and continued without looking at Johnson. "Shutup! I'm watching the debate…" The sergeant on the couch said referring to the current presidential election debate.

Rodriguez unhooked his tunic's collar while collapsing on the couch. He looked up a little too close to the TV and nearly toppled over backward recoiling from the sight of the morbidly obese debate moderator that asked the last question. Rodriguez exhaled, "Daaamn" in a low smart-assed voice. Like many physically fit people he pitied those who chose to be fat, and as a young man who declined 'political correctness' he did not feel that blowing sunshine up people's asses was virtuous.

Both young men were engrossed in the debate. The support of military personnel for the two presidential candidates favored the challenger, but not by the 100% Rodriguez hoped for. The sergeant thought that the military contained quite a few very average people simply seeking the greatest number of benefits for the least work possible who would therefore back the incumbent - President Mallory Winston - her socialist leaning redistribution policies, and her unceasing attempts to disarm law abiding citizens with ever more creative regulatory schemes. They even seemed willing to look the other way when her people covered up their various scandals pinning all justification on the shortcomings and misdeeds of past politicians, he thought.

On the other hand… *The Warriors*: the Marines, the special operations guys, the performers and anyone who cared about the U.S. Constitution and the sacred oath they had taken to defend it were supporters of the challenger. Both Marines giggled internally when they thought of their boss' infamous hissy fits and the severity of the tantrum she would throw if she saw them cheering her opponent on from the White House. The two were on the edge of their seats as the debate turned to the Benghazi controversy. The moderator apparently didn't care to follow this thread but the session had been scheduled to conclude with one more question from the audience.

A man in the audience was handed a microphone and he asked an obvious question; "Who was responsible for withholding the requested security from the American Ambassador in Benghazi and why was no one held accountable?"

Because it was the challenger's turn to answer first, he responded obliquely…"the day after the assassination of our American Ambassador to Libya…the first time this has happened… since 1979, in Pakistan… when we had four American diplomats killed…when apparently we didn't know what happened…" The governor knew that personnel in Benghazi had made accurate reports continuously throughout the attack, of course, but he wanted to give Mallory Winston the opportunity to trip herself up.

He continued…"The day after this attack…the President flew to Martha's Vineyard for a campaign fundraiser…this incident calls into question all of the President's policy in the Middle East… look at what's happened in Syria…in Egypt…now in Libya. Iran is now closer than ever to a nuclear bomb…the President's policies in the Middle East began with an apology tour" disdain in his voice "and pursue a strategy of leading from the rear…this strategy is falling apart before our very eyes." His allotted time ran out.

The moderator turned her attention to President Winston. "Your secretary of state…as I am sure you know…has said that he takes full responsibility for the tragedy in Benghazi. Does the buck stop with your secretary of state?"

"Our secretary of state has done an extraordinary job" she said melodramatically with little evidence to support the claim "but he works for me. I'm the President and I'm responsible" Ms. Winston delivered her line in the exact tonality she had practiced earlier. "The day after the attack, governor" she said to her challenger with a rehearsed glare… "I stood in the rose garden and I told the American people and the world that this was an act of terror and I also said we are going to hunt down those responsible for this." That wasn't quite true, of course. She had alleged that the militant's attack was a spontaneous riot in response to a YouTube video and before closing she *likened* it to a terror attack. The word 'terror' was used, but in a context that was designed to lead a listener to believe it was not *actually* a paramilitary attack.

She continued, "The suggestion that my secretary of state or anyone on my team would play politics with this is offensive" she said indignantly.

"Governor…if you would like to respond…" the moderator offered.

"I think the President just said something that is false. That is on the day after the attack she went in the rose garden and said this is an act of terror…you said in the rose garden that this was an act of terror? It was not a 'spontaneous demonstration'? Is that what you are saying?" The governor asked incredulously. "I want to make sure we get that for the record…" the challenger said, with raised eyebrows, knowing that the President's statement contradicted reality.

"Please proceed, governor… the President said with agitation in her voice.

"It took the President 14 days before she admit the attack in Benghazi was a terrorist attack…" the challenger stated. *Even then her people wove the fiction that we weren't certain what happened and it was unclear who was responsible for it* - he didn't bother to add.

"She did, in fact, sir" the moderator interrupted while the governor stammered, stunned that this moderator would violate the debate rules to help President Winston.

"Get the transcripts" Mallory Winston challenged now that she had been given breathing space and knew that it would not be done while they were on stage.

"She did, in fact, sir call it an act of terror" the moderator said incorrectly. The governor froze like a deer in headlights at the moderator's unexpected subterfuge in support of Mallory Winston's re-election bid.

"Would you say that a little louder?" Ms. Winston crowed, emboldened now.

"She did call it an act of terror" the moderator said more loudly as she had been commanded. She then attempted to soften the blow… "It did take, as well, a couple of weeks or so for this riot to come out…you are right about that…" the moderator's tone softened the misleading rebuke she had delivered while the words actually meant nothing.

"The administration indicated that this was a reaction to a video… a spontaneous demonstration…" the governor said, more quietly and circumspect now. He felt sucker punched, but he was sure this would be headlines tomorrow. The debate was carried on several channels after all and moderators from each of them had taken turns asking the questions. In the coming days he would struggle to understand why all media outlets but one failed to ask relevant and meaningful questions about the Benghazi cover up.

4.

G STREET

WASHINGTON, D.C.

9:45 P.M.

6 NOVEMBER 2012

Cadillac One, the presidential state car, pulled away from the White House and turned west on G Street heading out into the chilly night air. In the limousine's front compartment, a Secret Service driver scanned the edges of the street. The President's agent-in-charge of her protective detail sat in the front passenger seat communicating with the shift leader who was controlling the agents accompanying them in armored Suburbans.

In the rear compartment a small television displayed news from the cable network that helped President Winston win her most worrisome 2012 presidential election debate. They were tracking the national election results as they were reported. President Winston and her chief of staff for re-election Saleha Said were excited at how close victory appeared to be, but they were composed.

Saleha had been working a long time for this. She briefly reflected on the path she had taken to get here. Born in Michigan, and raised in Saudi Arabia, she respected her parents and they had encouraged her every step of the way. She had worked as an intern assigned to Ms. Winston when Richard Winston was the President of the United States and she managed to build that experience into ever greater positions of responsibility on Mallory Winston's projects. The President had even introduced her to her husband.

"...I'll get word to General Crassus' people tomorrow that you expect to receive his resignation..." Said said evenly.

"...Long overdue..." Mallory spat out, wishing she could get away with firing him. She had quietly relieved nearly a dozen generals that were not sufficiently excited about the "new direction" she was taking the country, but General Thomas Crassus was now her most loathed.

General Crassus had made a name for himself in Iraq. He was the commander of multi-national forces that chose to change strategic course. He made Marine General James Mattis' counter-insurgency techniques the standard for all forces in Iraq. The Iraq campaign's initial conventional objectives had been achieved with breathtaking speed, but that country quickly descended into anarchy fueled by former regime insurgents, jihadists drawn to the area for the opportunity to fight Americans, and covert Iranian influence operations.

The Mattis Strategy essentially turned the tide in Iraq creating a victory until President Winston unilaterally withdrew all American forces and the Iranians moved their surrogates in to fill the vacuum. None the less, Crassus had been immensely popular at the time he delivered success in Iraq and he had been appointed Director of Central Intelligence.

On September 11, 2012, the U.S. Embassy Annex in Benghazi, Libya had been attacked and overrun by a company sized force of islamist militants supported by RPG teams and mortar teams. Even the Ambassador was murdered. At the time the attack was going on - with CIA contractors onsite performing a hasty rescue mission and requesting assistance - Mallory Winston had decided that it was not necessary to assemble her crisis response team. In fact, it was Saleha Said that had convinced Winston that deploying forces to assist in Libya would provoke anti-Americanism and play into the hands of xenophobic racists in America. It would even give the impression that President Winston hadn't pounded the final nail into al Qaeda's coffin. Winston knew that there were some al Qaeda operatives participating in the attack...but there were members of other groups too...*who the hell knew what those savages were really ever after? What difference did it make anyway?* They had probably been wronged by a previous President she thought.

Online 'trolls' screamed that the President was guilty of negligence when she flew to Martha's Vineyard for a fundraiser in the morning. Later, when the Congress was trying to determine why administration personnel were pushing the ridiculous version of events that a protest gone bad overran the embassy, General Crassus was asked to have the CIA take responsibility for providing bad information. Obviously he could have been rewarded for assisting, but his assistance was lukewarm. He *thought* he was demonstrating loyalty to the Office of the President by not contradicting their claims and he was able to avoid lying, but Winston didn't have time for unenthusiastic underlings.

Like many powerful men, Crassus was fucking someone other than his wife. And like rulers going back to the time of Machiavelli and beyond, Winston made a very high priority of compiling information on the vulnerabilities of those around her. Now that the election was over, Said could have word delivered to Crassus. He would understand that he could resign and keep his damn mouth shut, retiring with all of his benefits intact and no action taken against him by the government or he could fight. Fighting would guarantee that the President would have the attorney general throw the weight of the government behind his prosecution. Crassus was on active duty. He was guilty of violating the Uniform Code of Military Justice. Indictments were rarely issued for consensual sexual adventures involving adults, but then the President was not generally motivated to weigh in in these situations.

"...It will be a very good riddance..." Mallory chided before being interrupted by a statement that riveted her attention.

The television host said soberly, "…We are now calling the election for Mallory Winston…Mallory Winston will continue to serve as… President of the United States…"

Saleha pressed a glass of champagne that Mallory had not even noticed her pouring into her hand. They toasted ebulliently. "…Forward…" she said, knowing the slogan would please the President. They both sipped.

Saleha slithered closer to Mallory and smoothly slid in a long provocative kiss. Mallory Winston may not have been particularly attractive to Aliyah Saleha Said, but beautiful women had long found ways to make powerful individuals attractive. Of course, Aliyah had a purpose.

Aliyah's father had served several islamist activist groups, but most importantly, he had been a devoted member of the Muslim Brotherhood. Her mother had also been involved in a number of islamist groups throughout her life. She had been the disciplinarian in young Aliyah's life. Even so, nothing but Allah's will could account for Mallory's ability to get her a Top Secret security clearance, Aliyah thought. Mom and Dad had raised little Aliyah for a very important mission. They had conditioned her to accept the necessity for *kitman* - deception for the advancement of Islam - in her life. They had disciplined her. They had given her the *Protocols of the Elders of Zion* and read the writings of Sayyid Qutb with her.

Just as al Qaeda was founded and led by Muslim Brotherhood alumni, so too were so very many other groups. Islamic terrorist groups founded on the ideology of the Muslim Brotherhood served as a deadly stick.

'Peaceful' subversive groups inspired by the ideology of the Muslim Brotherhood served as a poisoned carrot.

But right now, none of that mattered. Right now Aliyah was fulfilling her mission. Right now, Aliyah's hands penetrated the folds of Mallory's clothing caressing her and warming her for the pleasure that she craved - the pleasures that Aliyah provided. Cadillac One whisked the secret lovers ever closer to the private suite that would shield them from the memory of the White House guest logs.

EPILOGUE

PRESIDENTIAL PALACE

MOSCOW, RUSSIA

10:00 P.M.

6 NOVEMBER 2012

"**...N**o I'm not saying that...I'm not saying that at all...She is *not* a fool..." Nikolay Sludtsev said with an unusual level of animation. "...Mallory Winston may possess only an average intellect, but she doggedly focuses on what she wants and she can generally get it."

"What does she want?" Vladimir Putin asked. He was ready to dismiss Nikolay's observation before he clarified. There was no way a person could thread the needle of acquiring the most powerful position in America as an idiot. There were too many competitors. There were too many masters to serve for a fool to negotiate that journey no matter how cleverly they were stage-managed.

"...She wants her genius to be recognized. She wants power. She wants Americans to atone for their racist, sexist, colonial past and achieve 'social justice' by redistributing the ownership of resources in the present..." pausing, he added "...her biggest vulnerability is her total lack of historical awareness. She has no interest in the subject..." Nikolay conceded. "...I don't understand why, but she is insistent upon always giving Americans the impression that nothing is ever wrong... she is entirely unable to admit to any shortcoming of significance in anything or anyone under her control... even where you or I would recognize acknowledging reality as strengthening in the eyes of subordinates..."

He helped himself to Vladimir's bottle and poured some more vodka into his own glass before continuing. "My people looked at her more closely than anyone ever has...we had some work to do to clean her reputation up as far as voters were concerned...she saw herself as something of a revolutionary in her youth..." Old friends of the President had informed Nikolay's investigators that Mallory Winston literally had the clichéd poster of communist guerrilla Che Guevara in an olive drab fatigue cap complete with a red star on her dorm room wall. They described a girl caught up in the chic romanticism of communist revolution with no real understanding of the real-world context.

"...Her most notable accomplishment in law school was attending a trial for Black Panthers accused of torturing an FBI agent to death... you're familiar with this black militant group?" Putin nodded with disdain and Nikolay continued "She was present everyday as part of a law student monitoring committee attempting to chronicle anything that might be used to appeal the inevitable conviction...She interned with a committee working on the impeachment of President Richard Nixon, but was fired..."

"Why?"

"One of our sources said she falsified documents, another said she falsified the content of interviews", Sludtsev said.

"...Tell me more..." Putin said draining his glass and pretending to be inebriated as he had been trained to do as a KGB case officer so many years ago.

"...Through the Black Panther case she met attorney Max Mattel, the head of an American state level communist group,..." Putin found the American President's apparent empathy for Marxism to be wonderfully bizarre. He had been a member of the Communist Party of the Soviet Union for decades, but he didn't imagine communism to be a... a... *virtue.* It was just a tool for control...a means to exercise power and suppress dissent.

"...She interned with him after graduation. She failed the D.C. bar exam - the evaluation required to become a practicing attorney - but eventually passed a state bar and when her husband was elected governor she was hired on by an influential law firm based at the state capital..."

"...And we can count on her to suppress American energy production?" Putin said, trying to appear as unconcerned as possible when he broached his most important question. If fracking could be suppressed, Russian oil would remain a more potent form of gold. His European clients, dependent upon that oil, could never oppose him in any meaningful way. Russia would enjoy financial surpluses. Putin would lead the reconstruction of a magnificent empire. If, on the other hand, America drilled without hesitation, aggressively implemented the relatively new fracking techniques, produced coal to her maximum capacity and generally prioritized traditional energy development, she could see a financial renaissance of her own. At the very least, she would provide an alternate option for European energy consumers. Putin would lose his leverage. His nation would lose its path to wealth.

"...Absolutely. It is like a religion for her people. She has demonstrated no interest in critically analyzing environmental...*claims.* She is entirely unconcerned with seeing the scientific method practiced in regard to evaluating and implementing 'global warming' initiatives - no matter how dramatic. Creating a decisive narrative from international collections of individuals with the credentials of 'scientists' is sufficient to satisfy her curiosity.

Nikolay Sludtsev enjoyed another sip. He did not normally drink more than a glass or two of wine, and he certainly felt an internal glow right now. He was a man fulfilling his destiny. He had forged an alliance that made him a billionaire many times over. He *had* redeemed his father. His Free Community Partnership front groups had shaped a world markedly different from the one he was born into. Something as basic as American's 'melting pot' perspective - the belief that individuals willing to be productive, and voluntarily participating in a *free* marketplace could become citizens and prosper and depend upon persuasion to gain compliance or cooperation from others was erased entirely.

Without discussion, debate, or even a general awareness, his groups had positioned 'diversity' as the ultimate virtue. Diversity, as practiced, was a concept that provided the opportunity for a ruler to divide the whole, reward friends, punish enemies and consolidate power. Americans were now subdivided into groups that could be manipulated, combined, or isolated at will. Nikolay first controlled their perception and now he was going to control their reality. Sludtsev's fronts were the majority donors to eight of the ten most prestigious journalism schools in the United States. His people were on their boards. Over recent decades he had refined an ingenious system to reward media executives and personalities that carried the right messages and disincentives for those that strayed too far with interest in unconstructive questions. There was really only one major news outlet that resisted his enticements any more. Online, his people controlled the majority of the progressive blogs.

Persuasion was old-fashioned. Mandate was more efficient. Americans would never voluntarily atone for the past sins of their nation. Now...willingly or not, they would live in parity with the rest of the world. A wrench turner on an assembly line in Detroit was not going to live at a higher standard than a medical doctor in Africa. Human nature - as embodied in politicians - combined with a little direction from Nikolay's people had saddled America with sufficient debt that those debts could *never* be repaid. The collapse of the dollar was a certainty now. The dollar's status as the universal reserve currency was going to be brought to an end, and with it, America's enslavement of the world.

Nikolay Sludtsev was improving the world and he would be rewarded by becoming the wealthiest man on earth. His success was at hand. He owned one of America's two political parties and he wielded enough influence through key individuals in the other that there would be no coherent defense against his initiatives. Decades ago he viewed himself as positioning in front of coming trends. No longer. He was a man of destiny. He now took credit for *causing* the major trends driving current events. It was only natural that he would be positioned to ride the wave he created.

Vladimir Putin fingered his glass giving the impression that he was drinking much more than he actually was. Unlike Mallory Winston, he *was* a student of history. He not only studied Marx and Lenin, but Genghis Khan and the collapse of the Roman Empire. He too was a man of destiny and nothing was going to stand in his way. Yuri Andropov had entrusted him with a sacred mission in defense of the Motherland. That mission... and the elite status it gave him...sustained him through life. He would reconstitute the Soviet empire. He would build a more efficient, more effective, more powerful force. He would bring The Main Enemy to her knees.

With no further action taken he was confident that in less than a decade Americans and Europeans would no longer believe in the concept of private ownership of property - an idiotic paradigm that Russians had already rejected. Environmental regulatory compliance would trump all. He would be the man that finally constrained America.

And he knew where he would start. He had taught Georgia a lesson that would keep that tiny country in check for now, and he could return to them later. His next target was the Ukraine. When the time was right, the Crimea would be an easy grab. Mallory Winston would never go to war over that - not against a force that could make her pay a real price for intruding. Her response would let him know how quickly he would be able to take the rest of what he wanted. If she *didn't* go to war, Putin *knew* that a new Russian Empire was his for the taking. Today was a great day.

"Za fstryé-tchoo…" Putin hissed and violently downed the drink.

COMING SOON

Election: The Great Game in the Age of Unrestricted Warfare

ABOUT THE AUTHOR

Chris Graham is the former commander of a military anti-terrorism unit and is a former intelligence officer. He is the editor of The Counter Terrorist magazine. He is also a consultant and the creator of 30-10 training (www.chrisgrahamauthor.com).

Made in the USA
Middletown, DE
12 November 2014